SHADOW ASSASSIN

SHADOW SEALS

ELLE JAMES

TWISTED PAGE INC

SHADOW ASSASSIN

SHADOW SEALS

New York Times & USA Today
Bestselling Author

ELLE JAMES

AUTHOR'S NOTE

Enjoy other military books by Elle James

Delta Force Strong
Ivy's Delta (Delta Force 3 Crossover)
Breaking Silence (#1)
Breaking Rules (#2)
Breaking Away (#3)
Breaking Free (#4)
Breaking Hearts (#5)
Breaking Ties (#6)

Visit ellejames.com for titles and release dates
For hot cowboys, visit her alter ego Myla Jackson
at mylajackson.com
and join Elle James's Newsletter at
https://ellejames.com/contact/

CHAPTER 1

WHAT THE HELL had he gotten himself into?

Dane "Striker" Ryan adjusted the bowtie at his throat and stared around the *Baie des Anges* reception hall of the Hotel Le Negresco in Nice on the southern coast of France. He'd never worn a bowtie in his life, never been to Nice and sure as hell couldn't afford to pay the room rates at the hotel. If he'd had any other choice, he wouldn't be a fish out of water, dressed in a monkey suit walking into a highly publicized event attended by world leaders from all over the globe.

No, he'd be with his SEAL team, training or performing vital missions in some of the most godforsaken locations in countries these world leaders hailed from.

His chest tightened into a hard knot.

The only reason he was in France and not

homeless on the streets of San Diego was because he'd been given what he hoped was a second chance, an airline ticket and a wad of cash he couldn't refuse.

The offer couldn't have come at a better time. On the verge of being evicted from his apartment because he couldn't pay the rent, he'd been desperate. His job flipping hamburgers for a mom & pop burger joint hadn't earned enough money to keep a roof over his head. His years of training with the Navy SEALs meant nothing in the civilian world. The only jobs he was suited for required a clean record.

His record was shit. Dishonorably discharged from the military, he couldn't get employment washing dishes on a military base or in any government facility. He sure as hell couldn't get on with any security firms, providing armed escorts to diplomats or the rich and famous.

What else was he good for? He'd never held a desk job, his truck had been repossessed and he'd been facing homelessness. He'd been sitting at McP's, nursing a beer in the middle of the day while the rest of his team was gainfully employed, probably training for the next mission, when he'd gotten the call.

That fateful call.

It had come through as an unknown caller on his cellphone. Usually, he ignored such calls. But he'd applied to a number of establishments, hoping for more lucrative employment. He hadn't been able to afford to ignore a single call. He'd used his last few bucks to buy a beer, which wasn't nearly enough to drown the pain of his unwarranted disgrace and subsequent removal from the only job he'd ever known and loved.

"Dane Ryan?" a female voice had addressed him as soon as he'd hit the receive button.

"Speaking," he'd said.

"I understand you're being evicted from your apartment at the end of the week."

He'd frowned and almost hit the button to end the call, but curiosity stayed his finger.

"Who's this?" he'd demanded.

"Someone who knows what you did to lose your job, and the people who gave you the order to do it and then let you take the fall for them."

That had his attention.

His eyes narrowed. "What do you know?"

"That you can't get work because of the black mark on your record, you barely have two nickels to rub together, you need a job that pays more than minimum wage to afford an apartment in San Diego, and your team called you Striker because you were the best sniper in the Navy SEALs."

"You seem to know a lot about me," Striker had said.

"I do," she'd said. "I know you grew up in the

foster care system, joined the Navy at the age of seventeen and made something of yourself."

"Who is this?"

"Someone who cares. Someone who knows the value of your training and commitment to doing what's right."

"Yeah, yeah. Whatever. Do you have a name?"

"You can call me Charley," she said.

"Okay, Charley," he'd said. "Why are you calling me, telling me things I already know?"

"Because I have a job for you."

Striker leaned forward in his seat in the corner of the bar. "I'm listening."

"Good. Be looking for a packet to be delivered to your apartment. You'll receive instructions in that packet. Money has been deposited to your bank account. You'll receive another payment upon completion of your mission."

"What kind of mission?"

"You'll receive further instructions." And she'd ended the call, leaving Striker with more questions than answers. Immediately following the call, he'd received a text from his bank that a wire transfer had been made to his account.

When he'd logged into his account, he'd found that thirty-thousand dollars had been deposited into his checking account. He had no idea what the woman wanted him to do for that money, and it worried him. Did she want him to kill someone?

He'd killed before, but never for money and only the enemies of his country. If the woman knew him at all, she'd know that he wouldn't commit murder, no matter how desperate he might be.

That had been the beginning of this wild ride.

He'd hurried back to his apartment to find the packet that had been delivered. It contained a passport with his image and a fake name on it, a first-class airline ticket to France and the address of a hotel. It had also contained a wad of cash, the name of a men's clothing store and a note to buy himself some nice clothes for the trip. More instructions awaited him at his destination. At the bottom of the packet was a burner phone.

Thousands of dollars, airline tickets to France and a fake passport couldn't be good.

Striker had almost bailed at that point.

The burner phone rang at that moment. He'd answered, ready to say he was out and she could take back all the money and stuff.

"You're wondering if all this is legit at this point, aren't you?" the woman's voice sounded in his ear. "You're probably thinking this isn't an honorable mission and wondering if I'm setting you up to put a hit out on someone. Am I right?"

"Yes, ma'am," he said. "This kind of money can only mean trouble."

"Or it means what you're being tasked to do is very important."

"I'm leaning toward trouble."

"I know you were tasked to assassinate the Russian in charge of Internal Affairs. The man responsible for the corruption of their police force and the deaths of a number of American diplomats and tourists."

Striker's grip on the burner phone tightened. How did she know? The mission had been top secret. "I don't know what you're talking about."

She chuckled softly. "Would you consider a mission to possibly save the world for a second chance at your career in the Navy SEALs?"

"You can do that?" On second thought, he shook his head. "No one can do that."

"I have connections," she stated. "As a show of faith, look out the window of your apartment."

"Are you going to show your face?" he asked as he walked across the bare room to the window and opened the blinds. Below, in the parking lot, sat a black four-wheel-drive truck with knobby tires, tinted windows and a decal of a frog on the back windshield. "My truck? You got my truck?"

She laughed. "It's yours, free and clear, no debt associated with the vehicle, if you agree to perform this mission."

Striker frowned. "Still feels like a hit, especially with as much money as you're throwing at it."

"It's not," she said. "I'm not asking you to kill anyone."

"What *are* you asking me to do?"

"Take the ticket, buy the clothes, go to France. You'll receive further instructions from there."

"But what if—"

She'd ended the call.

Striker had had three choices. One, he could ignore the woman and keep the money and his truck. Two, he could ignore the offer, return the money and truck. Three, see where the mission was going, save the world and keep the money and truck.

He'd followed the instructions, reluctantly, knowing he didn't have much of a choice. The money in his account and his truck could just as easily disappear as it had appeared. The woman had said she didn't want him to kill anyone. How hard could this mission be?

And here he was, dressed like someone important, inside the reception hall of a fancy hotel in France, rubbing elbows with world leaders and awaiting orders.

When he'd arrived at the hotel, the clerk had been expecting him—at least the man on the fake passport. He'd handed Striker the keys to a suite in the hotel on the fifth floor. The bellman had led the way up, carrying the new suitcase containing his new clothes. Once inside the room, he'd found a tuxedo hanging in the closet, dress shoes in his size, an invitation to a reception in the hotel and a note.

Wear the tux, go to the reception and receive your orders there. Good luck. Charley

Before he'd gone down to the reception, he'd spent time reading up on the web about the reception, the attendees and the political issues they were facing.

The reception was the beginning of a two-day energy summit. The biggest issue up for debate would be the natural gas pipeline scheduled for expansion from Russia to Germany. Striker had studied the players involved from Sergei Baranovsky, the Russian diplomat heavily involved in the negotiations for the pipeline, to the German Federal Minister of Economics and Energy, Hans Sutter. Japan's representative was a small man with salt-and-pepper hair, Hikosaburo Kono. Other representatives hailed from the United Kingdom, France, Italy and the European Union. The one person who had him most intrigued was the man who'd replaced the assassinated leader of Russian Internal Affairs.

The man Striker had terminated while still a SEAL.

His replacement, Anatoly Petrov, had a reputation as an aggressive negotiator and a ladies' man. He liked women, and he liked getting his way, even if it meant turning his back and walking away from the table.

Striker wasn't sure what he had to do with the

Energy Summit, and he wasn't sure how he was supposed to receive his next instructions unless the instructions had only been to wear the tuxedo and show up at the reception.

Surely, that wasn't all of it.

Charley seemed interested in his skills as a Navy SEAL.

Navy SEALs weren't normally dressed in tuxedos, attending diplomatic receptions with leaders of foreign countries. When he'd taken out the Russian in charge of Internal Affairs, he'd done it from the top of a building over a hundred yards away. He'd had his rifle packed up and moved out of the building before anybody really knew what had happened. He'd never been this close to a bunch of politicians, and he sure as hell didn't fit in.

Along with the tuxedo and the shoes, he wore the earbuds Charley had given him in his first packet of information back in the States. He carried the burner phone in his pocket and awaited some clue as to what he was supposed to do at the reception.

He stood near the entrance, having arrived early to watch as the guests entered. Based on the pictures from the internet, he'd picked out Hans Sutter, the German, the Russians Sergei Baranovsky and Anatoly Petrov, the Japanese representative, and Lorenzo Ricci, the Italian. Richard

Weddington, the United Kingdom representative, had yet to put in an appearance.

Movement at the door caught his attention. The UK representative and his wife stepped through the entrance, showed their invitations to the security guard manning the door and crossed the room to the bar where they ordered glasses of wine.

A raven-haired woman entered next, wearing a long silver gown that clung to her curves and rippled like mercury with every step she took. She smiled and handed the security guard her invitation. He frowned down at it for a moment, and then glanced up with narrowed eyes. She laughed and smiled more broadly, pointed at the invitation and said something Striker couldn't quite hear from where he stood. The security guard tapped his ear and spoke into his microphone. A moment later, he gave the woman a nod and she entered the reception hall.

"Striker, can you hear me?" a voice said in his ears, startling him.

He hadn't realized how focused he was on the woman who'd just walked in until Charley's voice sounded in his ear. The comm device was a two-way radio which meant Charley had to be there in France and was close enough for the signals to come through.

"Roger," he said.

"Are you ready for your mission?"

Irritation flared. "Depends on what the mission is," he said. "Although, the use of my combat training seems irrelevant in this monkey suit."

Her chuckle filled his ear. "It all will become clear momentarily," she said. "And by the way, you look stunning in that tuxedo."

Striker glanced around the reception hall, searching for a female possibly standing alone who was talking to no one in particular. There were several women who had accompanied their husbands to the event. Most of them were older, and all of them seemed to be occupied with other people, except for the one in the silver dress. She stopped to snag a glass of champagne from one of the waiters circulating through the room, smiling to thank him.

"Your mission tonight..." Charley said into his ear.

The woman in the silver dress turned at the same time, her mouth still forming a smile across her lips.

"—is to keep an assassination from happening," Charley concluded.

No, the woman in the silver dress did not move her lips. The elusive Charley couldn't be her. Somewhat disappointed, Striker looked around the room. "Whose assassination am I supposed to stop? And by the way, I recognize the irony."

"Good. I know you did your homework on this

event," Charley stated. "If you've been following the energy struggles between Russia and Germany, you know how important this summit could be. I received intel indicating an assassination attempt will be made on one or both of the Russian diplomats. An agreement must be reached at this summit, or the energy needs of Europe could be at risk. Climatologists indicate the coming winter could be one of the harshest in decades. Without the additional capacity the new pipeline could produce, and with the growing population in Europe, it could spell disaster if an accord is not reached."

"Any idea who the assassin might be?"

"Therein lies the problem. My intelligence reports it's the same assassin who has eliminated four of the five diplomats with connections to the Russian mafia. No one has seen the assassin to know who he is. I know that's not much to go on," she said. "The targets are the Russians. Have you located Sergei Baranovsky and Anatoly Petrov?"

"Yes, ma'am," he responded. "This summit concludes in two days. Do either of the Russians know that I will be looking out for them?"

"No, and they are not to know. We hope that in the process of protecting these two men you might reveal the identity of the assassin."

"And my cover for this operation?" he asked.

"You're an escort for Natalya Zotin, a United

Kingdom citizen of Russian descent, who speaks fluent Russian and translates for the Russian Minister of Energy and the Russian in charge of Internal Affairs. She should be entering the reception hall at this moment."

A woman with auburn hair and wearing a green dress stepped through the entryway, handed her invitation to the security guard and looked out across the room. When her gaze met his, she smiled.

"Red hair?" Striker asked, careful not to move his lips too much.

"That's her," Charley said. "I'll leave you to it."

"Does she know why I'm here?" he asked.

Charley didn't respond.

Great. He didn't know if this Natalya woman was another one of Charley's agents or if he was supposed to pretend to be a male escort. How he was supposed to keep an eye on the Russians while entertaining a translator was a mystery to him. With the Russians in his peripheral vision, he moved toward the redhead in the green dress.

As they converged on the floor of the reception hall, she held out her hands. "Ah, yes. You must be Daniel Rayne. I was told to expect a handsome man as my escort this evening."

"You must be Natalya." He took her hand in his and lifted it to his lips, pressing a kiss to the backs of her knuckles. The name she'd addressed him by was the one on the fake passport he'd received in his packet from Charley.

She arched a perfect eyebrow. "You're American?"

He nodded. "Yes, ma'am."

She spoke perfect Queen's English with only a slight Russian accent. The fine lines around her eyes and mouth were a subtle indication of her age. She had to be in her late forties or early fifties and aging well.

"Do you speak any Russian at all?" she asked.

He shook his head. "Sadly, no."

Natalya sighed. "Up to that point, you were almost perfect."

"I shall take that as a compliment." He offered her his elbow, slipped her hand through the crook and they turned toward the other guests in the reception hall. Striker spotted the two Russians standing with the German.

"I suppose I need to work," Natalya said. "Shall we?"

Following her lead, Striker stepped out across the floor and headed toward the Russians.

"I know they speak fluent German, and the German speaks fluent Russian. So, I only have to be close by in case someone else wants to enter the conversation. Which means, I won't be completely tasked all evening. I had hoped to dance. You do dance, don't you?"

Striker grimaced. "My dancing has been strictly limited to country western music. My dancing skills are in the form of the two-step and the waltz. I'm good for those."

She smiled. "I'll keep that in mind. I am not familiar with the two-step, but the waltz…it is beautiful, no?"

Once again, *Great*, he thought. How was he supposed to keep track of the Russians while he was dancing as an escort for the translator? At that moment, he wished he had a handgun, a rifle or a knife. At least, then, he'd feel like he was in his element.

The reception got into full swing. Natalya made her rounds, following the Russians around the room. Striker quickly realized the woman could translate in a number of different languages, including Italian, French, English and German.

"I'm learning Japanese," she said, "But I'm not proficient yet." The music started from the string quartet in the corner. Several songs were played before Natalya smiled and said, "That's a waltz, would you like to dance with me?"

He frowned. "Are you sure you can take the break from translating?"

She laughed. "Yes, for at least one song."

He nodded and held out his arms.

She stepped into them and placed a hand on his shoulder and the other hand in his palm, and he led her across the floor in a waltz. The music was different but the dance was the same, and he managed not to make a fool of himself in front of all the important diplomats. As they whirled around the floor, he took the opportunities he could to keep an eye on the Russians. In one turn around the floor, he noticed the woman in the silver dress approaching Petrov and Baranovsky. When she spoke, they turned and responded, stern faces softening into smiles.

"The woman speaking with Petrov and Baranovsky, who is she?" Striker asked. He spun Natalya around so that she could see the woman.

His dance partner's brow furrowed. "I do not know this woman, though I might have seen her before at another event involving Russian diplomats. She seems to be holding a conversation with my two Russian charges. It appears my translations services are not needed."

The woman in the silver dress laughed and laid a hand on Petrov's arm. She turned to the side and, as she did, Striker noticed a long slit in the side of her dress that exposed her leg from the ankle to halfway up her thigh.

His groin tightened.

She had a stunning figure and an equally stunning leg. When she moved again, he noticed something odd about the tone of her skin just below the slit's opening. Maybe it was a trick of the lighting in the huge hall, but there seemed to be a discoloration just below the top of the slit. Perhaps the discoloration and the flesh tone of her leg was an undergarment she used to smooth her shape, as he was aware many women did. Or could it be a strap holding a weapon against the inside of her thigh...?

He stiffened. Thankfully, at that moment, the waltz came to an end.

The woman in the silver dress hooked her hand through the crook of Petrov's arm and walked with him toward an arched passageway.

On Striker's initial inspection of the reception hall, he had followed different hallways and corridors to determine where they led. The one the woman in silver was headed down led out to a tropical garden. The beautiful woman could be going with Petrov for a private assignation surrounded by lush, flowering bushes and palm trees. Or she could be carrying a knife beneath her dress with the intention of assassinating the Russian in the darkness.

"If you'll excuse me, ma'am," Striker said. "I need to visit the water closet."

"By all means," Natalya said. "I need to powder my nose, as well."

He indicated the direction in which the ladies' room was located.

Fortunately, the men's room was on the opposite side of the hall, conveniently positioned along the same corridor that led to the hotel garden.

"One moment, please." Natalya tipped her head toward the taller of the two Russians. "It appears Sergei might be leaving the reception hall and Anatoly already has."

All the more reason for Daniel to hurry and catch up with Petrov and the woman in the silver dress. However, he stood steady and gave Natalya his attention.

"Since they're leaving the reception, there is no need for me to stay to translate. I find myself fatigued. I too shall retire." She patted his cheek with the palm of her hand. "Your services are no longer required."

He captured her hand in his and touched the backs of her knuckles with his lips. "The evening has been my pleasure."

"Mine, too," she said with a smile. "And you're quite good at the waltz. The escort service did well in sending you."

"You'll have to look into country western dancing to learn the two-step for next time." He smiled and waited for her to turn away. Once she did, he headed out across the floor toward the corridor leading into the garden. With no other doorways leading off the corridor, he didn't wait or check to see if they'd stopped along the way.

When he stepped out into the hotel garden, he

waited for his eyes to adjust to the darkness. His ears perked as he listened for sounds at the other end of the dimly lit area.

Once his night vision adjusted, he eased away from the chateau and followed a pathway, walking as lightly as he could in his patent leather shoes. He followed the sound of voices.

Before he'd gone more than twenty yards, he saw the two silhouetted against the stone wall at the rear of the garden.

Striker stopped within twenty feet of them. He could reach them quickly, if needed. Instead of rushing the couple, he paused and watched. For all he knew, it could be a lovers' assignation. A tryst in the garden, away from prying eyes.

Petrov turned and gripped the woman's arms.

She reached up in an attempt to pry his hands loose from her arms. Her voice turned from a conversational tone to a higher pitched, strained nature.

"*Nyet*," she said and rattled off something in Russian. She tried to break free of the man's grip on her arms.

When Petrov still hadn't released her, her tone dropped low, the intensity increasing. A flash of movement brought her hands up through the middle of his arms, breaking free of his grasp. She grabbed his head, turned her back and flipped him over.

Petrov landed flat on his back.

In the next second, the woman had a knife pulled, the blade glinting in the moonlight.

Striker raced forward.

The silver-clad woman said something fast and furious in Russian as she held the knife over the man lying splayed out on his back.

Striker reached the woman before she could plunge the knife into the Russian's neck. He grabbed her wrist and yanked it up behind her back.

"Damn it, let go of me," she muttered.

Striker put his lips near her ear. "Ah, my dear, I found you finally. I believe they're playing our song. Shouldn't we be dancing?" He pretended to just take notice of the man on the ground. "What's this?" He frowned down at the Russian. "Sir, have you fallen?"

The Russian grunted and struggled to get to his feet.

With his free hand, Striker reached down and gave the man a hand up.

The woman he held with the arm up behind her back stood straight, unmoving, her chin tipped upward in defiance.

As the Russian stood, he brushed leaves from his suit and glared at the woman in silver.

"Are you okay?" Striker asked. "Do I need to call for medical assistance?"

The Russian shook his head. "*Nyet*, I am quite fine," he said in his stilted English. "Is this your woman?" He jerked his hand toward the woman in silver.

"Why, yes," Striker said. "I came to get her because I'm ready to leave. Are you ready to depart, my dear?"

She gave him a narrow-eyed glance out of the corner of her eye.

Using her body as a visual barrier, Striker removed the knife from her hand, folded the blade and slid it into his pocket. He lowered her arm to her side and slipped a hand around her waist, his grip firm. "Please, sir, allow us to see you back to the reception hall."

The Russian adjusted his suit. "I do not need assistance to find my way back." He turned and walked back toward the building.

Striker guided the woman in silver behind the Russian, giving him several yards of distance between them. Once the Russian reached the reception hall, Striker came to a halt, stopping just short of the building. He turned the woman around and lightly gripped her arms. He stared down into eyes as black as the night, the only light in their dark depths that of moonlight reflected off their liquid surface. "Who are you and why were you trying to kill the Russian?"

She spoke in Russian.

He shook his head. "English."

Again, she spoke in Russian.

"I heard you curse in English. Talk, before I turn you over to the security guards."

She stared up at him through narrowed eyes. "He attacked me. I was only defending myself."

"Sure, and you always carry a knife to diplomatic receptions? How did you get that past the security guards and metal detectors?"

She lifted a narrow shoulder. "A woman has to defend herself."

Her English held no trace of an English accent; it was American.

"You speak American English. Are you American?"

The woman crossed her arms over her chest, tipped back her head and stared down her nose at the man. "What's it to you?"

"Let's just say that I like to know my enemies."

"Am I one of your enemies?" She arched a black wing of a brow.

"I don't know. Are you?"

Her eyebrows dipped. "Only if you've done something to hurt me or my family."

"And is that what Petrov has done to you?"

Her mouth firmed into a thin line. "Perhaps."

"Do you make it a habit of trying to kill those who hurt you or your family?"

"No, but if he hurts me again, I will defend myself."

"In this case I will give you the benefit of doubt. In what capacity are you here?"

"I could ask the same of you."

"I'm here as a paid escort. And you?" He waited for her response.

"Translation services."

"Your name?"

She lifted a narrow shoulder and let it fall. "Alexa Sokoloff."

The name didn't ring a bell. None of the people who were attending the reception that were in the news had gone by that name. He'd have to put Charley to work discovering all there was to know about the raven-haired beauty. In the meantime, he'd do well to watch his back lest she plunge a knife in it.

CHAPTER 2

ALEX GAVE him the name she'd assumed since her parents' death. It had been a name on one of the passports they'd made for her. They'd kept a safe hidden behind a wall in the kitchen pantry where they'd stored passports from over a dozen different countries with as many different names on the passports and thousands of dollars in different currencies from the other countries. Should their cover be exposed, they had to be ready to pick up and move at a moment's notice.

Their final assignment had been in Russia where they'd attempted to provide their daughter a stable environment as they'd worked as sleeper agents from the time she was twelve until she was almost twenty-eight.

Images of that fateful evening flashed through her mind, hardening her heart and her determination. Two years had passed since she'd lost her parents. During those years, she'd focused on retribution. She was getting close to discovering the man behind their hit order. Nothing and no one would stop her from avenging her parents' deaths, not even this man in the tuxedo she'd noticed from the moment she'd stepped into the reception hall.

He'd been hard to miss. A dark-haired, handsome man, mingling with the paunchy, gray-haired statesmen from the attending countries was bound to stand out. Not that she was there to flirt with the attendees of the Energy Summit. She was there to get the final piece of information she needed to nail the one responsible…the one who'd given the order to terminate her mother and father.

"If you turn me in to the security staff," she said to the man in front of her, "I will tell them the same thing I told you. I was defending myself."

"And it will be your word against Petrov's. Who do you think they'll believe? A foreign diplomat or a woman nobody knows?"

Alex bristled. She might be a nobody. It didn't make her less of a person. Her parents had made a lifetime of being nobodies and yet they'd infiltrated the Russian government and had become trusted servants to various politicians. During that time, they'd fed information back to the US government as members of the CIA.

"What were you doing in the garden with Petrov to begin with?" the stranger asked.

She tipped her head up and stared straight into his eyes. "He asked me to come see the hotel garden, not that it's any of your business. Now, if you'll excuse me, I'll rejoin the reception."

"And I'll accompany you," he said.

"That won't be necessary. As you are fully aware, I can defend myself."

He lightly cupped her elbow. "I'm not so concerned about your safety so much as I am for the safety of the guests at this reception."

"You have my knife, and it's sharp so I wouldn't sit while it's still in your pocket. And it is one of my favorites. I would like it back before I leave France."

"You'll have to tell me where you're staying, and I will return it, after the diplomats have dispersed to their own countries."

She allowed the corners of her lips to turn up in a tight smile. "I am staying here at the chateau, like the rest of the guests at this reception."

"All the more reason for me to keep this knife."

She shrugged. "Whatever. I need to get back. My services might be required."

"Something you might have considered," he said, "before you attacked Petrov."

Her lips pressed into a thin line. "He attacked me and, if you were watching, you would have seen that." She pushed her shoulders back and stared up at him. "You know my name. What is yours, so I can retrieve my knife once the event is over?"

"Daniel Rayne."

She studied his face. He didn't look like a Daniel. "I'd like to say it's been a pleasure meeting you, only the jury's still out."

His lips twitched. "Trust me, the pleasure would be all yours."

She moved to go around him.

He dropped the hand on her elbow and stepped into her path.

"I'm unarmed," she said in clipped tones. "I'm not a threat to anyone."

He chuckled. "I'm not so certain about that, not after seeing how you threw Petrov over your shoulder like he didn't weigh two hundred pounds."

"I've had lessons in self-defense. A woman can't always hide a knife in her clothing."

"You managed to quite nicely, which is surprising as tightly as that dress fits your body."

Her cheeks heated. She chose to ignore the fact he'd noticed how her dress hugged her figure. With one eyebrow cocked, she asked, "And what is your connection to this reception?"

His lips spread into a smile. "I'm an escort."

She laughed. "I should have known."

His brow wrinkled. "And why should you have known?"

"I mean, look at you." Alex waved a hand at him. "You aren't old enough to be one of the politicians or delegates. You're too good-looking to be one of the scientists, and your moves are too skilled." Her eyebrows dropped and her eyes narrowed. "You're too skilled to be just an escort. I'd venture to guess you're more of a bodyguard or additional security hired by the chateau or some of the attending diplomats."

His grin broadened. "So, you think I'm good-looking, huh?"

"That's all you got out of what I just said?" She rolled her eyes.

"It's nice to know the suit is working."

Alex tilted her head to one side and studied him anew. "If you were part of the chateau's security team, you would've already turned me in as a potential threat, therefore I'll mark that off my list."

"And your self-defense techniques are too well-honed for you to be simply a translator," the man in front of her said. "So, what else are you? A spy? A call girl?" His gaze narrowed even more as he pinned her with his gaze. "Or an assassin?"

Her tight lips eased into a sultry smile. "I'm a translator," she said, "and you're keeping me from my duties. Now, either you move, or I scream."

He held out his arm. "Allow me to escort you back to the reception hall."

"I can get back there on my own," she reminded him.

"I know that, but I don't trust you to follow me in. You might be hiding another knife under that silver dress. I'd venture to guess you probably wouldn't trust me to follow you in, considering I still have the knife with which you tried to kill Petrov."

She frowned. "I was not trying to kill the man. He just needed to understand that no means no."

Daniel's lips widened into a grin. "Or *nyet* means *nyet*."

"If you were close enough to hear me say that, you were close enough to know what was going on."

Still, he held out his arm refusing to move until she took it.

"Fine." Alex hooked her hand through his elbow, and they started toward the reception hall moving down the long corridor.

The arm under the tuxedo sleeve was thickly muscled. The man's chest was broad and probably as muscular as his arm, making her feel small next to him. As she'd noted, he'd easily disarmed her when she'd been holding the knife over Petrov's chest.

She'd been angry with Petrov for grabbing her and refusing to let go. She had not intended to kill him, yet. Her intent had been to reinforce the idea that not all women wanted to make love with him.

Alex had briefly toyed with the idea of holding him at knife point to get the answers she wanted about who had given the kill order for her parents. It was probably just as well that Daniel had stopped her before she had gotten to that point. Her anger might have been her downfall and exposed her as the phantom assassin responsible for the deaths of a number of Russians, including the team that had been sent to kill her parents, and the middle-men who'd passed along the order.

One government official who had passed that order along, a man her parents had worked closely with for many years, someone they had trusted as a friend, who'd been to their house and shared meals with them, had been their Russian contact when they'd first come to Russia.

Alex might have spared him when she had gone to question his role in her parents' death, but things hadn't worked out that way. He had been surprised to see her and apparently scared, afraid that she knew too much and could expose him to the government officials with whom he worked closely. More than that, he seemed afraid someone would find out she hadn't died in the fire that had consumed her home and parents.

When he'd attacked her, she'd had no other choice. The man she'd considered a family friend had become just another puppet to the one who'd given the order to kill her parents.

Thankfully, they had met at a quiet place by a river. She suspected that he had chosen that location for easy disposal of her body. It had served that purpose, but she had disposed of his body in the river instead.

Anatoly Petrov had been his boss. Alex knew from all her research that Petrov reported to the President of Russia. He also had connections to the Russian mafia that dealt in a number of illegal activities, including human trafficking and drug trafficking. Alex suspected the mafia was also involved in siphoning off natural gas, selling it to other sources in Russia and to other countries.

Petrov wasn't the one calling the shots. Though Alex had been tempted, she wouldn't have killed him until he'd given her the name of his connection to the mafia and the one ultimately responsible for putting the hit out on her parents.

The team that had performed the hit had not been Russian military or Russian police. They had been a highly trained mercenary team, their payment source a Swiss bank account.

Alex had established several contacts on the Dark Web, who were still working on who owned those Swiss bank accounts. She didn't hold out much hope that it would lead to one individual. Those accounts were carefully buried in a number of organizations that appeared legit on the surface. In the meantime, she had to follow her own leads, thus her interest in Petrov and potentially, Sergei Baranovsky, another cog in the government wheel and potentially part of the Russian mafia.

"I noticed you with Natalya earlier," Alex said as they neared the reception hall. "Won't she miss you and be a little concerned when you show up with another woman on your arm?"

"So, you were watching me?" he said with a smile.

Irritation burned in her chest. "It's part of my job as a translator to read body language and to study the people around me."

He cocked an eyebrow and stared down at her. "What did my body language say?"

"You were only there to be polite to the older woman, and you were also studying the people around you."

"Natalya might be older than I am, but she is still a beautiful and vital woman and in the same *profession* as you."

Alex shot a glance in his direction. The way he'd emphasized the word profession made her blood boil. She had suspected Natalya did more than translate. She managed to be at every political rally, diplomatic reception, and government-sponsored event. Where there were government officials of the Russian country, she could always be counted on to be there in beautiful, expensive dresses and jewelry.

Most translators didn't get paid enough to afford that kind of couture. Several options came to mind on how she'd attained the wealth needed to wear that kind of jewelry and clothing. Natalya had received gifts of jewelry and enough money to keep her in the lifestyle to which she had become accustomed. She could have traded something other than her translation services for the items, or she had a source of income other than translation services.

"My services are limited to translation," Alex stated firmly. She'd many of the same political rallies and government functions as Natalya over the past year that she'd been building her own reputation as a translator. However, Alex had never traded her body for money or jewelry and had no intention of starting.

The self-defense lessons were for when she got into those situations where her clients or other people tried to take advantage of her. She then quickly reminded them that she was paid for her translation services not for any other skills they assumed she possessed.

Daniel stopped short of the reception hall entrance and put his hand over hers on his elbow to keep her from withdrawing it. "What's your story, Alexa?" he asked. "You speak fluent Russian, and yet, your English is purely American. Why are you really here?"

She smiled tightly up at him. "I am using my translation services to support myself. And you can call me Alex."

"Alex, when you're not in France, where do you live?"

"Wherever the work takes me," she said. "London, Paris, Moscow, the United States."

"You have no family, no children, no husband?"

Her smile faded into a tight line. "I have no family. It makes it easy for me to travel around the world. What about you?" She refocused attention on him, deflecting it from herself. "I take it you don't speak Russian?"

"Guilty," he said.

"Do you at least speak French, since you're here in France?"

He shook his head. "I am relying strictly on my good looks, as you called it. The pay and accommodations are decent. I have no complaints." He reached up and tugged at his tie. "Although, I'm not a big fan of ties."

She used that opportunity to slip her hand from the crook of his elbow. "And when your looks fade?" she asked.

"Then maybe I'll go back to the States, buy a ranch, settle down and raise a few kids."

She shook her head. "I can't see that."

He raised his eyebrows. "No?"

"You seem too cocky and sure of yourself to be relaxed."

"From what I understand, ranching is not a relaxing occupation. If I work during my good years and save enough money, maybe I can afford to have somebody else do the ranching for me. I can enjoy my time with my children and my wife."

"And you already have these children and a wife?"

"No," he said with a shrug. "But maybe someday."

Her stomach fluttered. She could imagine being the wife of this man who was cocky and sure of himself. She wondered if he would be the same in the bedroom. Heat coiled low in her belly. She stepped away from him as a natural reaction to keep from being burned. "Well, Daniel, I wish you well on your ranch with your wife and children. It wasn't a pleasure to meet you, but I do wish you luck in your *profession*," she said, emphasizing the word.

He chuckled. "And I wish you luck in yours, as long as it doesn't include assassinating Russian diplomats."

She kept a poker face and pasted a smile on her lips. "I'll do my best not to…unless they deserve it."

He laughed out loud. "In which case, perhaps we

should warn the Russian government you're on to them."

She almost hated leaving the man. He tempted her and kept her on her toes. She would do well to keep an eye on him during the course of the two-day event. She still wasn't convinced he was just an escort. The man's moves were fluid. He'd handled her like a trained combatant. His big hands, firm on her wrists, and his broad, muscled shoulders were clear evidence of a life of discipline and training.

"I suspect we'll meet again," he said.

"Perhaps," she said, and moved away from him.

As she stepped out into the reception hall, she heard a scream. Alex automatically ducked.

Daniel grabbed her around the waist, pulled her behind a wide column and then leaned out to view the crowd on the reception hall floor.

Alex ducked beneath his arm so that she might see as well. "What's happening?"

"I'm not sure," he said. "They're gathered around someone on the floor."

"Well, we can't find out who it is unless we get out there with them." Alex pushed past Daniel.

Daniel gripped her hand and hurried into the melee with her.

Some guests scattered, while others gathered around. A couple of the security guards pushed their way through the diplomats. The crowd parted as the guards reached the center.

Alex's breath caught when she identified the man lying on the floor.

Petrov lay with his hand clutched to his chest, blood oozing from between his fingers.

"Looks like someone got the job done," Daniel said beside her.

"Apparently not," Alex drawled. "He's still alive." She spotted Sergei Baranovsky and pushed her way through the crowd to him.

Daniel followed close behind.

When she reached the Russian, she spoke in his language. "What happened?"

"I was on my way out the door when I remembered I needed to talk to Anatoly. He was just coming in from the garden and headed toward the bar to get a drink, when a group of people moved between us. A moment later, he was on the floor. Apparently, someone stabbed him."

In that moment Alex was glad Daniel had her knife in his pocket. If they'd found it on her, she would've been hauled off to some French police station and held for questioning throughout the rest of the Energy Summit.

"Look," Sergei said, "he's getting up."

Petrov reached a hand up to one of the security guards.

The guard shook his head.

Petrov barked an order to him in French.

The security guard shrugged, gripped Petrov's hand and helped him to his feet.

The Russian was still bleeding as he clutched the wound on his chest, but he nodded, smiled at the crowd and spoke in Russian. "I'm okay," he said"This incident will not keep me from my duties at this summit."

At that moment emergency medical technicians pushed through the crowd with a wheeled stretcher.

They urged Petrov to lie on the stretcher.

Petrov insisted on sitting up, refusing to lie down. He allowed them to wheel him out of the reception hall as he shouted over his shoulder in Russian, "I will be back."

As they wheeled him toward the door, security guards had already set up a blockade, banning anyone from leaving the reception hall.

A French policeman arrived and stood in front of the onlookers, speaking to them in French, and then in English. "Please remain calm," he said. "Be patient as we investigate this incident. No one will be allowed to leave until we have interviewed everyone."

Alex turned to Daniel who was annoyingly close to her. "Good luck explaining that knife in your pocket."

"What knife?" he said with a grin.

She frowned in his direction. "What did you do with it?"

"Let's just say somebody else will have to explain why they have it in their pocket."

"Whose pocket?" she asked.

"Sergei Baranovsky," he said with a grin, "your Russian friend with whom you were just conversing."

CHAPTER 3

STRIKER HAD STOOD beside Alex as she'd spoken to
Baranovsky in Russian and while the French police
officer briefed the crowd. After Sergei turned and
walked away, Striker leaned close to Alex. "What
did he say?"

"Someone stabbed Anatoly Petrov. He didn't see
who did it." Her gaze shifted upward to the corners
of the reception hall.

Striker's gaze followed hers, and he noticed the
surveillance cameras.

"If you're one of the security personnel, you
should be able to view the surveillance videos."

He shook his head. "I told you, I'm not one of
the security team, but there might be someone I
can tap to gain access to those videos."

"We're on it," a voice said in his ear.

Charley.

Striker had almost forgotten the communications device through all the drama.

"We're reviewing the footage now," Charley continued. "A laptop will be delivered to your room. Hopefully by the time it reaches you, we will have access to the videos from the *Baie des Anges* reception hall. We'll download them to the laptop."

As Striker listened to Charley's voice, Alex stared at him, her eyes narrowing. "Is there something wrong with you?"

"Not at all. Why?" Striker asked, assuming his most innocent expression.

Sergei had followed the emergency medical technicians toward the exit only to be stopped temporarily by the French police where they patted him down, searching for weapons. Striker held his breath, waiting for the policemen to find the knife in Sergei's pocket.

When the police officer allowed him to pass through the door, Striker turned to Alex frowning. "Could he have found it that quickly?"

"Maybe he had a hole in his pocket," Alex said.

Hans Sutter, the German Minister of Energy was next to attempt to leave. When police officers noted his name on an electronic tablet, another checked his passport while a third officer patted him down, stopping when he reached the front right pocket of his trousers. The German frowned fiercely when the French policeman stuck his hands into the man's pocket and pulled out a knife.

Alex swore softly.

Striker recognized it as the knife that he'd taken off her. While Alex had been talking with Sergei, Striker had slipped the knife into Sergei's pocket. He only hoped that Sergei would touch it and smear their fingerprints, making them indiscernible.

It took several hours for the French police to get through the entire crowd in the reception hall. Other than the knife they found on the German, it appeared as though the actual weapon used to stab Anatoly hadn't been located.

Striker and Alex were some of the last people to make it out of the reception hall. Though he was impatient to get back to his room and the potential viewing of the video from the reception, Striker didn't want to appear too eager. He didn't want to leave and give the French police any reason to suspect him.

When they were finally cleared to leave the hall, Striker headed for the elevator. Halfway across the lobby, he was surprised to see Alex keeping up with him.

"Is your room in this wing of the hotel?" he asked.

She shook her head. "Not actually. You said that you might have access to the videos from the surveillance cameras in the reception hall. I want to know what's on those."

"So, you think by following me, I'll allow you to watch them?"

She shrugged. "It's worth a try."

"Considering you almost killed the man," he pressed the button to go up and waited for the door to the elevator to open, "I would've thought that you'd know who attacked Petrov. Aren't you two working together?"

A bell rang, and the door slid open. He entered.

She stepped in beside him. "I told you, I'm an interpreter. I was only defending myself. I wouldn't have stabbed my knife into Anatoly Petrov. I need him to remain alive. I also need him to understand the boundaries. No means no."

"I do believe he understands by now. Perhaps he was making a pass at another woman after he failed with you. She might've had the same self-defense training as you."

She ignored his comment. "Hopefully, the surveillance videos will shed some light."

Striker pressed the button for his floor. "Who would want Anatoly Petrov dead?"

"I can imagine any number of people, especially those people who don't want the pipeline project to move forward."

"And are you one of those people?"

She shook her head. "The people of Europe

need that natural gas. They have to get it from somewhere. Russia just happens to be the number two exporter of natural gas. It makes sense to purchase it from Russia. Meanwhile, Europe needs to be researching alternative fuel sources. It's unfortunate the German has been detained because of that knife. Nord Stream's Pipeline #2 originates in Russia and will culminate in Germany."

"Then why would Sergei put the knife into Hans's pocket? He would have as much at stake in this game as Anatoly, would he not?"

"One would assume so," Alex said. "But sometimes in Russia, the only way to get ahead is to trip your peers. Or in this case, kill them. Anatoly is in charge of the negotiations. If he's unable to complete those negotiations, Sergei would step up and fill his shoes."

"If that were the case then why did he set up the German who's on the other end of that negotiations table?"

"Perhaps he has plans to save the day, get Hans out of jail and then make him beholden to Sergei by freeing him to attend such an important summit meeting." Again, she shrugged. "This is all conjecture. Knowing who plunged the knife might give us a better idea of who's calling the shots."

The bell rang, and the door slid open. Striker waved his hand. "Ladies first."

Alex stepped out of the elevator and waited for Striker. He turned right and led her down the corridor to his room, wondering what he'd find inside and knowing that Charley had access. He waved his key in front of the door lock. Alex started forward.

He put his hand out. "Me, first."

She frowned but stepped backward.

He pushed the door open and flipped on the light. Everything appeared as it had when he'd left, with the exception of a laptop lying on the desk. After a cursory check in the bathroom, he waved Alex inside. When she hesitated at the door, he gave her half a grin. "Afraid I might pull an Anatoly?"

"The thought did cross my mind."

"Trust me, I think I'm more afraid of you than you are of me." He sat at the desk and powered up the laptop. It immediately came up on a screen with the image of the reception hall and the approximate time of the incident. It appeared to be before the actual stabbing occurred.

Alex joined him at the desk and leaned over his shoulder looking at the video. "Like Sergei said, he was speaking to Anatoly moments before the stabbing," Alex said. And there, a group of people moved across between Sergei and Anatoly as Anatoly left to go to the bar. Half a dozen individuals blocked the cameras view of Anatoly. The video switched to one from a different angle. "How did you do that?" Alex asked.

"I didn't," Striker said.

"So, you aren't just an escort, you're part of the security team, are you not?"

He shook his head. "I am not. I just have friends." Which was a lie. All he knew was the voice of a woman who called herself Charley. She could have been the one out there on the reception hall floor plunging her knife into Anatoly's rib cage. For that matter, she could have sent Alex to distract him and to make Anatoly more careless and unsuspecting when he returned to the reception hall. As the video played, Daniel watched Alex through his peripheral vision. Was she actually watching to make sure that the deed was done, and that the actual person who stabbed Anatoly wasn't visible by any of the surveillance cameras?

The same incident replayed from the opposite angle. Striker zoomed in on Anatoly. Several men in tuxedos stepped between him and the camera, and they seemed to be laughing down at someone else. Striker couldn't make out the person, considering they were looking downward. It had to be somebody shorter, possibly a female. He glanced at their legs hoping to catch sight of another pair of legs or the skirt of a dress, but nothing seemed clear, and the two men in the tuxedos weren't close enough to Anatoly to plunge a knife into the man's body. In the next second, Anatoly was down. Some of the people who had clumped around him continued across the reception hall floor unaware of the man who had fallen to the ground. "Do you know any of these people around Anatoly?" Striker asked.

Alex pointed at the screen. "The man in the lead is the Italian Minister of Energy. The one beside him is his aide."

They slowed the video down and replayed it several times, zooming in on the people surrounding Anatoly. They looked at it from all the angles the cameras had to offer and came up with nothing. Any one of those people who were close to Anatoly could have been the one who had stabbed him.

Striker figured he should be doing this video review on his own but there was something about Alex that he trusted, even though she'd held a knife over Anatoly's body. It was strange because he had no reason to trust her. He didn't know her. He didn't know what she wanted, but she seemed just as determined to find out who wanted Anatoly dead. Striker turned to her. "Why do you care?"

"I have my reasons," she said.

"Is it because you wanted to kill him yourself?" he asked.

She propped a fist on her hip. "If I had wanted to kill him, I would've done it as soon as we walked into the rose garden. I only pulled my knife to reinforce the fact I didn't appreciate his intentions. The French police will be reviewing the video surveillance," Alex said.

Striker nodded.

"And they'll come up with the same conclusion we have. We still don't know who struck Anatoly Petrov. It could've been anyone in that group," Alex said. She drew in a deep breath and let it out on a sigh. "Fortunately, the strike wasn't sufficient to kill the man."

Whoever had done it still had two days to complete their mission, which meant that Striker had to be on his toes for the next two days. He wasn't sure how he would mingle with the diplomats as a paid escort. Alex had the better vantage point as a translator. She would be involved in all the sessions discussing the fate of the pipeline and the other items on the agenda for the energy summit. Unless he offered his services as a bodyguard to the Russians, he might not be able to infiltrate the conference room where the diplomats would be discussing the fate of several nations and their access to natural gas.

"I'd better be going," Alex said and headed for the door.

"I'll walk you to your room," Striker offered.

She shook her head. "That is not necessary."

He dipped his head in acknowledgement. "I

know you can take care of yourself; however, I wouldn't be much of a gentleman if I didn't offer to see you to your room."

She smiled. "I would prefer if you didn't."

"Very well," he said, "then I'll call it a night." He walked with her to the door, reached around her to open it and held it as she walked through.

She turned and faced him. "I wasn't going to kill Anatoly."

The sincerity in her tone and the expression on her face made Striker want to believe her. But he didn't know her, and he wasn't sure if he could trust her. Still, his instincts told him he could. He didn't like her walking around the hotel by herself at night even though the hotel security was pretty tight. They hadn't stopped the attacker from stabbing Anatoly. "I'd rather you let me walk you to your room," Striker said.

"I would rather you didn't. Goodnight, Daniel," she said.

Hearing her calling him Daniel was jarring to his senses. That was his cover, and he had no intention of blowing it. "Goodnight, Alex."

She turned and walked toward the elevator. He stood in the hallway until she entered the car. When the doors closed, he ran down to the elevator bank and watched as the elevator rose two floors to the seventh. He punched the button to go up. He wasn't sure why, she had specifically said for him not to follow her, but his gut told him to try. A different elevator rose. He waited and watched as the elevator she had gotten onto paused for a long time on the seventh floor before finally coming back down. Meanwhile, the other elevator's door opened.

Striker stepped onboard and punched the number seven. The door slid closed, and he rose up the two floors. When he stepped out into the corridor it was empty. Short of knocking on each door until he found the right one, he'd missed his opportunity. He stepped back through the opened elevator door and went back down to his floor. When he entered his room, he couldn't help but feel how empty it was without her presence. He sat at the desk and brought up the images on the laptop and ran through the recording several more times before concluding the videos were useless at positively identifying the person who had stabbed Anatoly Petrov.

"Well done tonight, Striker," a voice said in his ear.

He jumped, not having expected somebody to be talking to him at that time of night. His heart beat hard in his chest. "Charley, you've got to stop popping into my ear."

She chuckled. "My apologies for startling you."

"How can you say I did a good job?" Striker said.

"I was busy out in the garden with a woman while one of the Russians was attacked."

"Without being a personal bodyguard," she said.

"Well, I didn't protect Anatoly from an attack."

"Even had you been in that reception hall," Charley said, "you still might not have protected him from an attack. No worries," Charley said. "However, we did perform a background check on Alexa Sokolov. We were able to capture her image when you two were viewing the video footage from the *Baie de Anges* reception hall."

Charley had his attention. "And?"

"Her parents were CIA agents who were exposed and murdered in Moscow two years ago. Alexa was believed to have perished in the fire that burned their home to the ground. Apparently, she didn't."

"Does she have any other siblings?" Striker asked.

"No," Charley said, "she was an only child."

"What does she do for a living?" Striker asked.

"She was a translator before her parents' deaths."

Striker snorted. "She claims she's a translator now. That jives with her story, except for one thing. I found her in the garden about to stab Anatoly Petrov. She swears she wasn't going to kill him. She was just using the knife to send a message to the man to keep his hands off her."

"She bears watching," Charley said. "I'll have my people go deeper into her background."

"What about Natalya?"

"Your duties for her ended. She only needed an escort for the reception."

"If I am no longer a paid escort, how do I maintain my cover?"

"The sessions are heavily monitored, and you won't be allowed into those. However, they don't go on all day long. The delegates will have to adjourn for lunch and for the evening meal. Lunch and dinner will be provided in one of the banquet halls. You'll eat when the delegates eat."

"Yes, ma'am," Striker said.

"Oh, and, Striker, move about with caution and keep your eyes open. My sources assure me tensions are high and the stakes are higher."

CHAPTER 4

ALEX TOOK a circuitous route back to her room on the third floor of the hotel, going up first to the seventh floor and back down to the third in case anyone was watching or following her.

Having traveled and worked alone for the past two years she'd learned various tricks for maintaining her anonymity and guarding her own safety.

Using her various passports, she'd bounced back and forth between the United States and Russia. In the U. S. she'd taken the time and invested in lessons in Israeli self-defense techniques, and she contracted several survivalist former special forces groups who trained civilians in combat techniques. She had learned to fire a number of different weapons and had strategically placed a variety of weapons in multiple locations in the United States, United Kingdom, Germany and Russia.

Her parents had left her a significant amount of money, making it unnecessary for her to get a job after their deaths. They had invested well and had Swiss bank accounts only she could access in the event of their demise.

All the information she'd needed had been on a flash drive, backed up on a compact disc and stored in a safe along with her passports and the money. They'd understood the risks of raising a child where both parents worked with the CIA. Though she'd long been out on her own, working as an interpreter, using their home as her base when she had to travel, her association with them had put her at risk. If their cover was ever blown, she would be in danger.

They'd taken care of their only daughter financially, if not emotionally. Fortunately, they'd insisted she learn a number of different languages. Not only was she fluent in Russian and English, she also spoke German and Italian. They had left her with connections to people who could provide her with passports, as well as computer gurus who were fluent in navigating computer databases and hacking into just about any government or mafia computer system. Although the pain of loss had faded over the two years, she still missed her parents and wished she had spent more time with them and paid more attention to the people with whom they'd worked.

When she arrived at the door to her room, she waved the keycard in front of the lock, pushed the door open and looked inside before stepping in. Her father had taught her to always look before she stepped into any situation. She'd only barely understood the importance of that advice upon their deaths. The house where they'd lived in Moscow had been designed with an escape route built into the kitchen pantry.

The night her parents had died, she'd gotten home from her job well before her mother and father. She'd been in the kitchen making a pot of tea when she'd heard the front door slam open.

Alex had hurried to the living room to see what was wrong.

Her father slammed the door shut and pushed a table in front of it.

"What's wrong?" she'd asked.

Her father had reached into the desk beside the door and pulled out his pistol, dropped the magazine from the handle, checked it and pushed it back into the weapon.

Her mother turned to her. "Ally," she'd said urgently, "go to the pantry." When Alex had hesitated, her mother spoke more urgently.

She hadn't moved, a rush of apprehension

rippling through her body. "If something's happening, I want to be with you."

"Go, now," her mother insisted. "Get to the pantry, there's a flash drive in the safe. Take it and get out of here."

"But—"

"We've been over this many times when you were a child. You can't stay. We need you to get that flash drive and get out of here." Her mother crossed to her, cupped her cheek with her hand and pressed a kiss to her forehead. "We love you. Now, go!"

"Hurry," her father had said. "They're coming."

"Who's coming?" she'd asked.

Something had crashed against the door. The door frame splintered but held.

"Ally, go!" her mother had said, her tone stern, her eyes filling with tears as she took another gun out of the desk drawer and aimed it at their front door.

In the next moment, the door to their home crashed open. Alex turned and ran to the pantry. The sound of gunfire reached her ears through the thick paneling of the pantry door.

Every instinct in her body had told her to go back out and fight for her parents. But what could she have done? She hadn't had a gun. Though her father had taken her out into the country and taught her how to fire his 9 mm Glock, she hadn't been comfortable with it.

The gunfire had sounded more like automatic weapons, machine guns. Though it tore her heart apart she'd pulled hard on the pantry shelf that worked as a hidden doorway. Opening it quickly, she'd stepped inside a dark and narrow stone-lined passageway.

Behind her the gunfire had ceased. The sound of furniture crashing and glass breaking, led Alex to believe that they were looking throughout the house for any others that might be hidden. They must have known to look for her. The safe containing the passports and money had been stored in that passageway. She'd grabbed the flashlight hanging on a hook on the wall and spun the safe's tumbler. Her fingers had trembled so much that she hadn't gotten the safe open on the first try. Before she'd worked the numbers again, smoke had filtered through the cracks in the wall of the pantry. Before too long, the smoke had been too thick; she'd had to leave.

She'd been down that passage many times with her father as he'd schooled her on where to go in the case of someone storming their home. When she'd been younger it had been a game, like hide and seek. As she'd grown older, it became a way for her to sneak out to meet her friends. It hadn't mattered how stealthy she'd been, her parents had always known when she'd gone out and had been waiting for her when she returned. They'd never chastised her but hadn't slept until she was safely back home.

The night they were murdered, she'd run down that passageway that led beneath the street and angled upward through a drainage grate into the garden of a Russian Orthodox church.

From there, she'd crawled up onto a wall and watched as flames filled the night sky from the home she'd known for fifteen years, knowing deep down her parents had not made it out alive.

If they had, they would have followed her along the passageway. The fire had burned through the night until there was nothing left of the house but rubble. The smoke had cleared before sunrise. Alex had covered her mouth and nose with her shirt and felt her way along that passageway back to the safe. By the beam of the flashlight she'd carried with her, she'd rolled the combination lock right then left then right again and opened the safe.

Her parents had always left a backpack beside the safe. That night she'd learned why. She'd filled the backpack with the contents of the safe, zipped it hurriedly, left through the passageway and emerged into the garden.

She'd wandered the streets of Moscow for days, wearing a knit cap, her hair tucked inside, her face down, refusing to make eye contact with anyone. If the people who'd killed her parents had known she was alive, they'd have come after her to finish the job.

Alex had found an abandoned warehouse and set up camp. She'd used internet cafés to catch up on the news. Her parents' death had been nothing more than a blip on a newscast. Family perishes in a housefire. She'd also used the computers to tap into the flash drive her mother had been so insistent she safeguard.

At one point, she had thought she should notify the CIA of her parents' deaths, but if she had then they would know that she was still alive. If the CIA knew she hadn't perished in the house fire, whoever had put the hit out on her family might find out as well. She'd decided it was best that she had died in the fire, for all intents and purposes.

She'd gone through all the information in the backpack. She'd found a US passport with her image on it and set up a plan to get back to the United States. With enough Russian rubles to get her out, she'd caught a train and headed for a port where cruise ships disembarked.

At the port, Alex had found her way into a warehouse containing pallets with supplies for the cruise ships. In the wee hours of the morning, she'd hollowed out one of the pallets to make sufficient room for her to fit inside. The pallet had been staged the night before to go on the next cruise ship. In the morning, a forklift had lifted the pallet and driven it onboard the ship. The tricky part had been getting out with nobody seeing her.

Fortunately, the receiving area had been somewhat chaotic with a multitude of pallets being driven onto the ship, offloaded and set aside. The cruise ship had left Moscow with her on it. Eventually, she'd made it back to the States, bought a used car with cash, stolen a license plate and had driven to the hills of Idaho where she'd begun her training. She never again wanted to feel as helpless as she had the night her parents had died, and she'd vowed to make the people who'd killed them pay.

Tired to the bone Alex stripped out of the silver dress, stepped into the shower, washed off her makeup and the hairspray and let the water run over her face and body, rinsing away the tension of the night. She stepped out of the shower, dried off and slipped into the leggings and T-shirt she preferred to sleep in at night. She slid her feet into the slippers the hotel had provided, liking the feel of warm terry cloth wrapped around her toes.

Just as she was about to open the bathroom door, she heard a noise in the other room. It sounded as if somebody had broken glass. She dimmed the light then opened the door a crack, just enough to see a man reaching his hand through the broken glass to unlock the French doors opening onto the balcony.

Alex didn't have time to think, she only had time to react. In her slippered feet, she raced across the room.

Just as the man shoved the door wide, Alex plowed into him like an American football player. She slammed into him hard enough that she drove him backward until the backs of his legs hit the railing. He flipped over backward and would have fallen the three stories to the ground but, at the last minute, his hand grabbed hold of the top of the rail. The gun he'd been carrying clattered to the ground. He hung for a moment by one hand.

Using her fist, Alex pounded those fingers hoping he would let go. She needed something harder that would hurt him. However, she reasoned that by the time she'd found something he would be back up on the balcony after her. The man was big.

Alex knew her limits.

She ran back through the French doors, closed and locked them. It would only slow him down a little, but maybe enough to allow her time to get away. She ran through the room, grabbed her backpack and her shoes and raced out into the corridor. A dining cart with the remains of someone's meal stood outside one of the rooms. Alex grabbed it and pushed it in front of her door then raced for the stairwell. She could have gone down to the lobby to report that someone had broken into her room, but that would be first place he'd look for her.

Hopefully by the time the attacker made it out of her room, he'd think that she'd taken the elevator down. Years of keeping a low profile told her to go up the stairs instead of down. As she raced passed the elevator, she punched the down button. Then she dove for the stairs, pushing through the door, letting it slam shut behind her.

Alex ran up the stairs as quietly as she could in her slippers. Fortunately, she traveled with everything she owned in a backpack. Sometimes, she stored important information in lockers at the airports that she traveled to most. Mostly, she lived out of her backpack, purchasing items she needed in the places she visited.

As she climbed the stairs, she wondered where she would go. Her first thought was of the American on the fifth floor where she had been earlier. Below her, the stairwell door on the third floor crashed open. She slowed, only to make her movements quieter and eased up the stairs to the fifth floor. Footsteps sounded on the stairs below. They seemed to be fading, as if whoever was running was heading down to the ground floor instead of up.

Alex waited a few seconds to make certain that was the direction he was headed, and then quietly pushed the stairwell door open onto the fifth floor. Once she'd passed through it, she eased it closed behind her. Unfortunately, she couldn't control the loud click of the latch engaging. If her pursuer had heard the same click, he'd be headed back up the stairs. She only had moments to hide somewhere. She ran down the hallway to the door she had entered earlier and knocked three times. With her heart pounding against her ribs she waited, praying the man had not gone to sleep.

"Daniel," she called out softly. "Please, open the door." She positioned her face in front of the peephole, counting the seconds. She'd just raised her hand again to knock when the door swung open.

Daniel stood there with a frown denting his brow. "What the—" he started to say.

She pushed him backward far enough to let the door swing shut behind her then she leaned against it breathing hard, her pulse racing.

"You want to tell me what's going on?" Daniel demanded.

Alex nodded. "Let me catch my breath first." She sucked in air until she'd secured enough in her lungs. When she had control of her pulse, she pushed away from the door, turned around and glanced through the peephole.

"Is someone after you?" Daniel asked.

"Shhh," she said. "Yes. He broke into my room." She gasped as a man dressed in black ran past the door. She turned to Daniel, pressed a finger to her lips and mouthed the words, *He's out there now.*

Daniel leaned in and pressed his eye to the peephole, and then jerked back.

"He's still there, isn't he?" she asked in a quiet whisper.

Daniel nodded, pulled her away from the door and into the bathroom and spoke in a soft voice, "Stay here." When he moved to go around her, she grabbed his arm.

"What are you going to do?" she asked quietly.

"Look," he answered.

She didn't release his arm, her fingers tightening. "What if he has a gun?"

His lips quirked upward. "Then I won't stay long." He leaned closer and whispered in her ears. "I'll be back."

Alex waited in the bathroom as he stepped out and once again pressed his eye to the peephole. He remained there for several very long seconds. Then he shook his head and looked her way.

"Is he gone?" she whispered.

He shrugged. He moved to the other end of the room where he pulled the drapes across the window and turned off the lights. Once again, he returned to the door and looked out the peephole. Again, he shook his head. "He could be gone. The only way to check is to open the door."

Alex shook her head. "If he's anywhere on the

floor, he'll follow the sound of the door opening. Just leave it. He'll go away." Alex left the bathroom and checked for herself through the peephole. As Daniel had indicated, nobody stood outside the door, but the man could be anywhere on that floor, or he could have moved on to the next floor up. If he'd been going down, he wouldn't know what floor she'd got off on. Hopefully, he'd give up and go away. In the meantime, Alex was stuck.

"Might as well have a seat," Daniel said softly. He waved a hand toward one of the chairs beside the doors to the balcony.

She shook her head and paced, adrenaline still pushing through her veins at an alarming rate.

"Why would somebody want to attack you?" Daniel asked.

Alex shook her head. "Maybe Petrov didn't like being bested by a female?" she suggested.

"Especially if he thinks you had anything to do with his stabbing."

She nodded. And if it wasn't Petrov, then who? Though she looked very much like her mother, her mother had gone prematurely grey. Alex's hair was still jet black like her father's hair. When she'd first come back to Russia, she'd worried that somebody would recognize her. She'd returned as an American interpreter, easily finding work because of her excellent grasp of the English and Russian languages. But it was a possibility that somebody had recognized her as Anya, the daughter of Pavel and Mischa Federov. She'd assumed the name Alexa Sokolov, from the US passport she'd found with her picture on it.

"So, what now?" Daniel asked. "Do you want me to contact the front desk and ask them to send a security team to escort you back to your room?"

"No," she said. "I don't like to draw attention to myself. This summit is not about me. There's already been enough drama with Petrov's stabbing, which you know I did not do."

"That would have been kind of hard for you, considering you were with me."

She nodded. "Which is probably just as well that you disarmed me. If I'd been caught with that knife on my person, I would've been the one detained instead of the German Hans Sutter. For that matter, if he's not released by tomorrow, I won't have a job. I'm here to translate for him."

"How did the attacker break into your room?" Daniel asked.

"He broke the window on my balcony's French door so that he could unlock it."

"And you just ran out of the room?" he asked.

She shook her head. "No, I charged him and knocked him over the balcony, but he hung on."

Daniel grinned. "The guy I saw in the hallway was no lightweight."

Alex stopped pacing and stared at him, her gaze

going from his head to his toe. "He was probably about your size."

"I'm impressed," Daniel said.

"I'd have been more impressed if he'd have fallen all the way to the ground. My room was on the third floor."

"Not the seventh?" Daniel cocked an eyebrow.

Alex's eyes narrowed. "You followed me?"

He shrugged. "I might have. Do you always go up in the elevator before you go down?"

She shrugged. "A girl has to be careful. It doesn't pay to let somebody follow you back to your room."

"Apparently, somebody found out where you were staying. I can't imagine anyone breaking into a random room."

Alex shook her head. "Me either."

"Which leads us back to the question, why you?" He raised his hand. "And yes, it could have been Petrov being embarrassed by a woman. But I get the feeling that you're not telling me something I should know. Who are you really?"

"I told you...I'm an interpreter."

"An interpreter who carries a knife and can flip a full-grown man over her shoulder. Right," Daniel said with a snort. "In what language training school do they teach that?"

"A girl has to—"

"Take care of herself," he finished. "You don't have much faith in people, do you?"

"Since my parents' deaths, I have yet to meet anyone I can trust," she said.

"And yet, here you are in my room."

"It was the only place I knew to go on short notice. I'll be leaving you now," she said.

"And go where?"

"That's not for you to worry about."

"But I will. Look," he said, "you're welcome to stay here." He raised his hands. "I promise not to touch you." A smirky smile curled one side of his lips. "Unless you want to be touched."

She pressed her lips together. "Believe me, I don't want you to touch me. I should go. I've already imposed on you too much."

He waved toward the door. "Then go on. Poke your head out there. He might still be looking for you. Your best bet is to stay put until daylight. Masked men in black don't usually show up in the daylight. I still think you need to report this to the front desk. How else are you going to explain a broken French door?"

"I'll worry about that when I check out." Still, Alex hesitated.

"The offer stands open. You can stay here. I'd say you can trust me but, seeing as you are not a trusting soul, you'll have to take your chances."

She stared at him through narrowed eyes.

He held up two fingers like a Boy Scout. "I do so solemnly swear to be a gentleman, but then again there are your trust issues."

Alex drew in a deep breath. She didn't have anywhere else to go, and she was tired. "Okay, I'll stay."

"You can sleep in the chair," he said. "Or you can sleep in the king-size bed with me. It's plenty big enough for two people."

"I'll sleep in the chair," she said, cutting him off.

CHAPTER 5

STRIKER WAS surprised when Alex agreed to stay the night in his room. He'd really thought she would leave and look for someplace else to sleep. Given the late hour and the fact that she'd have to let the desk know why she was moving from her room, he guessed she'd decided it made sense for her to stay with him.

He'd promised her he wouldn't touch her, and he'd stand by that promise even though his groin tightened at the thought of sleeping in the same room with the beauty. He guessed it would be a long night with little sleep for either one of them.

Despite having told her she'd have to sleep in the chair, he found himself saying, "You can have the bed. I'll sleep on the floor." He wanted to kick himself for offering, but he knew it was the right thing to do.

She shook her head. "No, thank you. I'll sleep in the chair. The floor is too hard for anyone to sleep on."

He chuckled. "I've slept on much worse."

She frowned in his direction. "I wouldn't think that escorts would have to sleep on floors very often."

Realizing his mistake, he backpedaled. "It happens," he said. His reference to sleeping on hard surfaces went back to his time spent sleeping on the ground or in foxholes as a Navy SEAL on a mission. He wasn't there as a Navy SEAL, and she didn't need to know that he used to be one. "Please," he said, "take the bed."

He dragged the comforter and one of the pillows off the bed, made a pallet on the floor and stretched out to prove he was sincere.

She stared down at him on the floor, a frown denting her perfect brow. "This is your room. It doesn't seem right for you to sleep on the floor."

"Nevertheless, I am. So, somebody ought to sleep in that bed." He laced his hands behind his neck and closed his eyes.

"How do you know I won't try to kill you in your sleep?" she asked.

"I pride myself in being a good judge of character," he said. "You don't strike me as someone who would kill a man in his sleep."

She snorted. "You are too trusting."

He opened his eyes and stared into hers. "And you don't trust enough."

Alex crossed her arms over her chest. "How do I know you won't kill me in my sleep?"

"If I had intended to kill you, I would have done so by now. As I am sure, if you had intended to kill me, you would have done so by now."

Alex kicked off the slippers she'd worn during her escape from her room and crawled into the king-size bed. As soon as she was settled, she was back out again.

"Did you forget something?' he asked.

"Yes," she said. "I like to keep a light burning. Do you mind if I leave the one on in the bathroom?"

"Not at all," he said. "I can sleep through anything and, at the same time, I'm a light sleeper."

The bathroom light was still on. All she did was close the door most of the way, leaving just a crack to let light into the room. She returned to the bed and switched off the light on the nightstand. Then she laid down in the bed and pulled the sheets up to her chin.

Silence stretched between them. A million questions ran through Striker's mind. He still didn't know much about this woman, other than her parents had been killed in a housefire. She might be telling the truth about being a translator, but she seemed to be more than that, and she wasn't telling him what that other part of her was. Then again, he wasn't telling her who he really was and why he was there. Still, the mission didn't define him, and he suspected it didn't define her either. "You speak fluent Russian. Where did you learn it?" he asked into the shadowy darkness.

For a moment, she didn't respond. Just when he'd thought she'd gone to sleep she said quietly, "My parents. They were born and raised in Russia and immigrated to the United States shortly after they were married and barely out of their teens. We lived in the Unites States the first few years of my life where I learned to speak both English and Russian. Then we moved to Germany. For the next few years, I went to German schools. Immersed in the language, I learned it quickly. Then my parents moved back to Russia where I went to Russian schools until I turned eighteen."

"So, you speak fluent Russian, German and English?"

"Yes, and I learned a little Italian while I was in the Russian school. I'm not as fluent in Italian, but I can get by."

"I'm impressed," he said. "And it makes sense to be an interpreter with your skill set."

"It does make it easy to find work," she said. "What about you? Have you always been a male escort?"

He snorted. "No, but it seems to be the only kind of work I can get now."

"What did you do before?" she asked.

"I worked in security," he said. Which was as close to the truth as he could say without blowing his cover. And he had worked in security. The security of his nation.

"Security? Hmm," she said. "You look to me like somebody who might have been in the military."

Her words struck too close to home. "How so?"

"It's in the way you carry yourself with a certain amount of pride. And you appear fit."

"You don't get too many male escort jobs if you don't remain fit," he pointed out.

"True," she said, "but it's really your bearing that sets you apart from others and makes me think that you've had military service in your background. Am I right?"

With her point blank question, he stumbled. "My father was in the military. He taught us how to stand tall and be proud of our armed forces and of our country. What did your father teach you?" he asked to deflect her attention from him.

She laughed softly. "He taught me to observe people and situations and to always be aware of my surroundings."

"That's a good thing for a woman to learn," Striker said.

"Actually, it's a good thing for anyone to learn. He also taught me how to learn from others and blend in wherever we lived. It makes it easier for me to assimilate to new surroundings."

"Where are your parents now?" he asked.

She didn't answer for a long moment. Then her voice sounded softly in the darkness. "They are deceased."

"I'm really sorry to hear that," he said. "How long has it been since they passed?" he asked.

"Two years."

"That's not long ago," he said. "You must still be hurting."

"I miss them, but life goes on. And you?" she asked. "Do you still have parents?"

"They're alive and living in Texas. Although it's been over a year since I've seen them."

"What's keeping you from visiting?" she asked.

He wanted to say pride. Instead, he said, "I've been busy trying to make a living."

"Don't wait too long," she warned. "None of us knows how long we have on this earth. You have to appreciate those you love while you can. I know I did. And every day that goes by I wish I still had my parents."

"I do miss fishing with my father," Striker said. "I miss the peace and quiet, and then the excitement of catching a fish. We always ate what we caught or released them back into the water. He's a quiet man, but in his silence, he teaches by example, showing me how to do things more than telling me, from baiting a hook to how to treat a woman. He loves my mother and would do anything to make her happy."

"My father loved my mother too, and my mother adored him," Alex spoke softly in the darkness.

"How did they die, if you don't mind my asking?" Striker said.

"They were murdered in our home."

Striker's chest tightened at the thought of Alex losing both of her parents so tragically. "Were you there?" he asked.

"I escaped; they did not."

"Was this in Russia?"

"Yes," she said.

"I'm surprised whoever killed them let you live."

"They didn't know I was there. I got out before they found me."

"I'm sorry, Alex. I know what it feels like to watch somebody you care about take their last breath. I can't imagine that someone being one of my parents. I'm sorry."

She gave a harsh laugh. "What do you have to be sorry about? You didn't kill them."

"No, but I feel your pain, and I've experienced it."

"You say your parents are alive. Who have you lost?"

"My brother," he said. It had been one of his

Navy SEAL teammates. He'd held him in his arms as he'd taken his last breath after sustaining a gunshot wound to his chest. Though Striker had gotten him out of the firefight and into the helicopter, the medic hadn't been able to keep him alive all the way back to the forward operating base. He'd died in transit, the wounds too grievous for the medic to stop the bleeding.

"I'm sorry," Alex said. "You must have cared deeply for him."

"I did." His teammate had been his brother in the most important sense of the word. If Striker could have, he would've taken the bullet for him so that he might live. "What did you do after your parents' death? Did you stay in Russia?"

"No," she said, "I made my way back to the United States. It was a little over a year before I returned to Russia."

"I'm surprised you came back to Europe at all," he said. "Why did you return?"

"I was able to get work as a translator."

"Couldn't you have done that in Washington D.C.?"

"Not as easily as I could in Moscow. And I guess I also needed to prove to myself that I could go back without fear."

"You say you're here as an interpreter for the German delegate?" Striker asked.

"Yes. Hans Sutter."

"But you weren't with the German minister at the reception last night."

She nodded. "My primary duties are for during the summit. I'll be there tomorrow throughout the day."

"Sounds to me like a long boring day of blah-blah-blah."

She laughed. "There will be a lot of that. Men in power tend to posture a lot, but hopefully, they'll get down to the business of determining the fate of the pipeline. It's why most of the people are here. Either they are all for the additional pipeline or completely against it. There doesn't seem to be a whole lot of middle ground right now. Hopefully, they can come to an equitable solution by end of day tomorrow. If not, it will bleed into the next day. I know the Germans, and many other nations within the EU, are anxious to contract for additional natural gas in anticipation of heating Europe through the winter. The increase in population is in part due to the growing communities of migrants who've been coming from war torn nations in the Middle East and in Africa."

"I understand from my reading," Striker said, "that the current flow of natural gas won't be sufficient to get Germany, or any other country within the EU, through the winter."

"That's right," Alex said. "In other words, it's very important for the Russians and the EU, in particular Germany because the pipeline will end there, to come to some agreement before the end of this summit."

"Which means the Russians and the Germans need to live long enough to make that agreement," Striker said.

"True."

Silence stretched between them, and for a little while Striker thought that Alex had fallen asleep.

Then her voice came through the darkness. "You don't strike me as someone who would appreciate being a male escort for long."

"It pays the bills," he said. "But you're right. It's not really my thing. It wasn't something I dreamed of as a boy growing up with my father who worked with his hands raising cattle on a ranch in Texas."

"Why don't you go back to Texas and work with your father?" Alex asked.

"I can't," he said. "Not yet. Not until I have proven to myself, and to him, that I can make it on my own."

"And after you've proven all that? Then what?"

"Then maybe I will go back and learn to be a rancher. I know my father would love that."

"And would he approve of you being a male escort?" she asked.

"My father would approve of anything that makes me happy."

"And does being a male escort make you happy?" she persisted.

"It pays the bills," he repeated. "What about you? Did you dream of being an interpreter as a little girl?"

She snorted. "No, my first dream was to be an Olympic gymnast, but I didn't start young enough, and we moved before I could get any good at it."

He chuckled. "And after you moved, did you come up with a new dream career?"

"I loved history. My father and I would read books together about people, places and different eras. It all fascinated me. I thought one day I might become a history teacher."

"And why didn't you do that?" he asked.

"After my parents' death, I realized I had to support myself. I didn't have the money to go to college, but I did have the skillset to be an interpreter. Many college students never achieve that level of understanding of different languages. It takes being immersed in that society where that is the only language you hear and use."

"If you could choose any other career, what would it be?" he asked.

"Anything that didn't require being around politicians and diplomats. Right now, working on a ranch with your father sounds pretty good. The fewer people I'd have to deal with, the better. Animals seldom talk back."

Striker laughed out loud. "They may not be able to talk back, but they get their message across. They can be just as stubborn as any human. I should know. I had a horse stand on my foot and refuse to move because he was mad I hadn't given him another bucket of grain."

Alex chuckled. "I would prefer that over any human any day."

"You'd prefer a horse to stand on your foot?"

"No, but I'd prefer to deal with an animal with an attitude than with a person with an attitude."

"I get that," he said. "People can be more complicated and rude."

"I still feel bad about you sleeping on the floor," she said.

"I'm fine," he said.

"You paid for this room. This is your bed. You should be sleeping in it."

"I'll rest peacefully knowing that you're comfortable," he murmured.

"And I'd feel better knowing that you were sleeping comfortably in a bed. There's plenty of room for both of us. This bed is huge."

Striker was tempted. "No. It's okay. The floor isn't that bad." He knew that if he climbed into that bed, he wouldn't sleep much at all, not when a beautiful woman lay beside him. One who had touched his heart with her memories of her love for her parents. He couldn't imagine being alone in a foreign country having to deal with the loss of his parents.

"I don't take up much room in this bed," Alex insisted. "I'd feel better if you were sleeping in the bed you paid for."

He started to say that he hadn't paid for it, but he couldn't. He shifted on the makeshift pallet. The floor was particularly hard, and the comforter did little to soften it. He sighed. "Okay, as long as you put pillows between us." He prayed that would be enough to keep him from rolling over in his sleep and gathering her in his arms. Afterall, that dress she'd worn earlier that evening had done little to disguise her incredible body.

He wouldn't get much sleep on the floor, and he sure as hell wouldn't get much sleep in the bed. At least he'd be more comfortable while he wasn't sleeping.

He climbed onto the bed and settled on the edge as far away from her as he could get. "Better?" he asked.

"Much," she said. "Now, I can go to sleep. Goodnight, Daniel, and thank you."

"Goodnight, Alex." He lay for a long time staring at the ceiling in the dim sliver of light making its way into the bedroom from the bathroom.

Not long after she'd said goodnight, Alex's breathing grew slower and deeper.

Striker lay in the dark, listening to every breath

she took, his body aching for something he couldn't have. He didn't know this woman, and he was there to do a job. And when the job was done, they'd part ways, never to see each other again. He found himself saddened at the thought. He turned on his side, his back to her. He closed his eyes and willed himself to go to sleep. But sleep wasn't easy to come by with a beautiful woman lying next to him. He was glad Charley would do a little more digging. Maybe she'd discover more about Alexa Sokolov.

CHAPTER 6

ALEX WAS surprised that when she woke the next morning she'd actually slept through the night, something she hadn't done since her parents' deaths, and despite the fact she'd slept with a stranger.

Daniel had promised not to touch her and though she had a natural distrust of everybody, she inexplicably believed him. The pillows had been more of a barrier to keep *her* from touching him.

They hadn't been necessary. She'd slept soundly and undisturbed. When she opened her eyes, she looked toward the other pillow beside her and found it empty. She sat up straight in the bed. The sound of a shower running in the bathroom reassured her that Daniel hadn't left.

With him occupied in the shower, she jumped

out of bed, hurried to her backpack and unearthed her wrinkle free blouse, jacket and the skirt she'd brought to wear when she was translating during the summit meetings. In the mirror over the dresser, she quickly combed the tangles out of her hair and applied a light coat of makeup. She was stepping into her shoes when Daniel emerged from the bathroom with nothing but a towel wrapped around his waist.

"Oh, good. You're awake," he said. "Room service should be delivering breakfast about—" A knock at the door interrupted his sentence. He grinned. "Now." He crossed to the door, checked through the peephole and turned to her. "It's room service."

Alex ducked out of sight as Striker opened the door. A member of the hotel staff wheeled in a cart and laid covered plates on the table in the corner. He wheeled the cart back out, and the door closed behind him.

"I wasn't sure what you wanted, so I ordered coffee, tea and espresso. You choose." He removed a stainless steel cover from one of the plates. "And I hope you like eggs Benedict. If you don't, they've also brought a variety of cold cuts and toast."

"If you don't mind, I'll have the tea and toast," she said. The scent of food made her tummy rumble.

"Good," he said. "I prefer coffee." He lifted the mug of coffee, took the top off, drank a long swallow then glanced at his watch. "You only have a few minutes before you have to be down at the summit meetings...?"

She nodded, nibbled at the toast and drank the tea.

"What are you going to do about your room today?" he asked.

"I'm not exactly sure. I suppose I could check and see if they have an opening for another room."

"You're welcome to stay here another night. I'm almost sure I heard them say the hotel was fully booked for this event."

"I've already inconvenienced you enough," she hedged.

"We've been through this argument." He held up a hand. "The offer's open."

"At the very least, I'd like to leave my things here until I decide what to do." She met his gaze. "What about you? What will you be doing during the day while I'm attending the summit?"

"I want to do more research on some of the players involved in this meeting, as well as review the video again in case I've missed something." He also intended to speak with Charley to find out what she might have learned.

"The summit will have a catered lunch in one of the banquet halls," Alex said.

"I'll be there," he said. "Though I'm not included in the summit meetings, I do have access to the luncheons and dinners."

"I hope you know I won't be sitting with you," she said.

He nodded. "It would be better that people don't know where you're staying, especially considering the attack last night."

"I would like to come up to the room at lunch, if possible."

"I can make that happen," he said.

"Just watch for me when I leave the banquet hall." She nodded, glanced at the clock on the nightstand and set her tea on the tray. "I'd better go." She hurried down to the large conference room where the summit would take place and took her seat beside the German Minister of Energy. He understood a little Russian and was fairly fluent in English, but he'd requested an interpreter just in case. That had been Alex's means for gaining entry into the conference. With a little help from a computer hacker, she'd made the top of the list for potential interpreters for the Energy Summit.

The summit meeting got underway with an introduction of all foreign leaders, scientists and decision makers. The representative from the European Union gave a brief history on the different types and origins of energy sources used throughout Europe.

He named the countries represented that provided those resources. He also talked about the continuing influx of migrants from Africa and the Middle East, and how the growing population in the EU had increased the demand for energy. The early forecast for the coming winter indicated it would be even colder than the previous one, and they were concerned about meeting their energy needs.

He then turned the meeting over to Anatoly Petrov, who segued into the need for the second phase of the Nord Stream pipeline to meet the increased demand for natural gas in Europe.

Even if Hans Sutter, the German delegate, didn't need it, Alex provided a soft-spoken translation of everything said.

After Anatoly had explained how the pipeline would be laid at the bottom of the Baltic Sea alongside the original Nord Stream pipeline, he took a seat looking pale, the injury obviously causing him pain.

As soon as Anatoly sat, Richard Weddington, the representative from the UK stood. "Adding another pipeline only emphasizes our dependence on nonrenewable energy. What are we doing to reduce our need for nonrenewable fuel?"

Anatoly struggled to his feet again. "Part of our plan for introducing the new pipeline is to also allow sufficient funds to continue research into alternative fuel sources."

"Assuming you put this pipeline in place," the German spoke in Russian, "are you prepared for the possibility of someone employing ransomware that could shut down the original pipeline as well as the phase two pipeline?"

Anatoly pressed a hand to his chest and winced. "Our team has developed antivirus software to block the deployment of ransomware into our system."

Weddington frowned. "You have software that can effectively combat ransomware? Has it been tested? Is it proven?"

Anatoly nodded.

"You have antivirus software, and you haven't shared it with everybody else?" Richard Weddington continued, his voice rising.

"It works with our upgraded computer system. We can retrofit the existing controls to work with the phase one pipeline. The point is, if this pipeline is approved, it will be foolproof and provide the millions of additional cubic feet of natural gas needed to keep Europe warm this winter and many winters to come."

"How do we know you're not working with the hackers that produce the ransomware? Everyone knows the hackers are Russian."

Sutter pounded his fist on the table in front of him, making Alex jump. "Share the antivirus software so that we know it is viable," he said. "Otherwise, you're no better than the people who produce the ransomware."

Anatoly's face turned red, and he swayed on his feet. "How dare you accuse me of producing ransomware and blackmailing nations. We export energy. We don't need to hold nations hostage." As quickly as his face turned red, it blanched white, and he fell back into his seat.

A security guard rushed forward and helped Anatoly to lie on the ground. He used his radio to call for help and, within seconds, the door opened and a stretcher was wheeled in. The medics lifted Anatoly onto it and wheeled him out. Some of the attendees stood, others remained seated.

Sergei Baranovsky held up his hand. "There's no need to disband this meeting. I'm here as backup to Anatoly Petrov. We can continue this discussion."

The moderator took control and stated that since it was near lunchtime they should adjourn until after the meal when they could continue the discussion.

The German rose from his seat so fast that his chair fell backward, slamming against the floor. His face was a ruddy red, his jaw set in a tight line. He muttered a curse in German and stormed out of the room. Others left frowning furiously.

Alex could hear them talking angrily amongst themselves. They were furious with Anatoly and the Russians for holding back necessary antivirus software that would keep hackers from employing their ransom software and effectively shutting down the delivery of natural gas and other energy resources to the nations that needed it to keep warm.

The other Russian interpreter stopped beside her as Alex gathered her things. "Quite the drama, don't you think?" she asked.

Alex kept a straight face. As an interpreter she refused to show emotion or take sides. "It is an interesting discussion," she said, trying to keep her comment neutral.

The older woman held out her hand. "I'm Natalya Zotin, the interpreter for the Russian delegates."

"Alexa Sokolov." Alex shook the woman's cool, slender hand.

"Are you interpreting during lunch?" Natalya asked.

Alex shook her head. "I'm only required at the summit meetings."

"Why don't you sit with me?" Natalya asked. "We can compare notes on what it's like to be an interpreter."

With no real excuse on the tip of her tongue, Alex nodded. "That would be nice." They followed the crowd into the banquet hall where tables were laid out beautifully with charger plates, fine china, and seven pieces of silverware at each place setting.

Natalya led her to a table where the Saudi energy representative sat with Hikosaburo Kono, the Japanese delegate. The other interpreter's choice immediately put Alex out of her comfort zone. She spoke no Japanese and no Middle Eastern dialects. Fortunately, Richard Weddington, the UK representative took the seat beside hers.

Natalya leaned forward and addressed the UK delegate. "Richard, it's good to see you again."

He nodded. "And you too, Natalya."

Their use of first names indicated a close familiarity with each other, and Natalya turned to Alex. "Richard, have you met Ms. Sokolov?"

He shook his head and held out his hand. "I have not had the pleasure."

Alex took his hand. "Nice to meet you, Mr. Weddington."

"Nice to meet you too, Ms. Sokolov. You're interpreting for Mr. Hans Sutter, the German Minister of Energy?"

She nodded.

Weddington's lips pressed into a thin line. "He appeared quite angry leaving the summit conference room."

She gave a tight smile rather than a response.

Another interpreter sat between Richard and the Saudi. The Saudi spoke to the interpreter, and the interpreter turned to Richard Weddington and introduced the Saudi. A conversation ensued between the UK representative and the Saudi representative, thankfully leaving Alex out of the conversation.

"So, Ms. Sokolov, or may I call you Alex?" Natalya asked.

"Alexa, and you can call me Alexa."

"I detect an American accent. Where did you learn to speak Russian and German so well?"

"In school," she said. It was her canned answer for people she didn't want to know her background. Her parents' secrets were her secrets.

"And where might that school be? I'd like to recommend it to others who might pursue careers in interpretation."

"Sorry, but the school is no longer in business." Another lie she'd grown used to using.

"Such a shame, especially when they did such a good job."

"What about you, Ms. Zotin?"

"I grew up in Moscow, and my parents moved me around quite a bit when I was young. We spent time in Germany, the United Kingdom, Italy, and even in Saudi Arabia." She smiled and nodded at the Saudi delegate.

He nodded in return.

"I became quite adept at picking up different languages and have made friends all over the world," Natalya said with a smile.

"How many languages are you fluent in?" Alex asked.

"Eight, and I'm able to adequately communicate in another six."

"That's amazing," Alex said.

Thankfully, the meal was served, and Alex wasn't required to talk while they ate. Alex picked at her food, pushed it around on her plate and finally set her fork aside.

"Is the meal not to your taste?" Natalya asked.

Alex gave a tight smile. "No, it's quite good. I'm just not all that hungry, and I need to get back to my room for a few minutes before the afternoon session begins."

"I need to go to my room as well. I'll walk with you."

That was not how Alex saw that happening. Out of the corner of her eye, she spotted Daniel making his way to the banquet hall doors. He glanced her way and gave a small, almost imperceptible nod.

Natalya walked with Alex all the way to the elevator.

Daniel hung back, letting them enter the elevator without him. Alex thought to punch the seventh floor. Instead, she entered three, the real number that she'd been assigned. As the elevator rose, she pulled her keycard from her wallet.

"Oh," Natalya said, "we're on the same floor."

Alex swallowed a groan as the door opened.

Natalya waited for Alex to emerge and didn't make a move until Alex turned in the direction of her room. They walked side by side. "Have you always been an interpreter?" Natalya asked.

"For the most part," she said. "You?"

"Not always. I've dabbled in business, but the corporate world was not for me. I'm happy doing what I do. I have more control over the work I take on."

Alex stopped in front of her door. "It was nice talking to you. I have a few things I need to do before I go back to the summit."

"Me, too. I'll see you there."

Alex waited for Natalya to move past her. When the woman didn't, she waved her keycard over the door lock. She pushed the door in just enough to get through it, and then turned and closed the door between her and Natalya.

The broken window was a glaring reminder of the evening before. Her pulse picked up. She stared around the room, half-expecting the man in black with the mask to show up again. She checked the room to make sure there was nobody else inside, and then went back to the door and looked through the peephole.

Apparently, Natalya had moved away from the door. She waited another three minutes before she pushed the door open and peered out into the hallway. It was empty.

Alex left the room and headed for the closest stairwell. As she pushed through the door, she looked back over her shoulder. The floor was still empty. She hurried through, let the door close behind her and then climbed the stairs to the fifth floor. When she opened the door to the stairwell, she heard another door clatter below. Alex muttered a curse beneath her breath. Hopefully, it wasn't Natalya following her. She walked quickly to Daniel's door and knocked three times softly. The door opened immediately, and she dove in.

"Are you all right?" he asked. "Is somebody following you?"

"I'm not sure," she said.

He leaned into the peephole, stared for a moment and then straightened. "Did you see who it was?"

"No," Alex said, "but I had an interesting lunch with your girlfriend."

"What girlfriend? Oh, you mean Natalya."

"Yes, she invited me to sit with her, and then grilled me."

His lips twitched. "Did she find out any more than I have found out about you?"

"She didn't get much further."

"She's an interesting woman," Daniel said.

"She is," Alex agreed. *And kind of creepy*, she thought.

"Was she following you?"

"I don't know...maybe. I told her I was going up to my room after lunch to do a few things before I went back to the summit. She said she also had to go back to her room. And then she got into the elevator with me. I punched the button for the third floor, and she said 'oh, we're on the same floor.'" Alex grimaced. "When I got out and went to my room, she followed me. It wasn't until I went inside my room and closed the door that I finally got rid of her. I waited a few minutes, then left the room and came up here. At the fifth floor stairwell door, I thought I heard somebody open a door below me. I could just be imagining things." But her gut told her she wasn't.

Daniel frowned. "Why would Natalya follow you?"

"Good question," Alex said.

"How did it go in the summit meeting?"

Alex filled him in on the discussion between the attendees and how Petrov and the German left the room.

Daniel shook his head. "A much more interesting morning than I had."

"Did you have a chance to look over the video again?" Alex asked.

"I did." Then he shook his head. "I didn't find out anything different."

"Did you learn anything else about the attendees?"

"I did some web surfing, but nothing seemed to indicate a motive for murder."

"Well, I guess I better get back to the summit. Are you still okay with me leaving my things here?"

Daniel nodded. "And I'm still okay with you staying here again tonight."

"Thank you," she said. "Can we discuss it later after the summit meetings and dinner?"

He nodded. "The offer remains open. I won't withdraw it, unless you turn out to be a real assassin."

She gave him a stiff smile. "I take it you're a man who likes to take risks?"

"Calculated risks," he said.

"I guess we'll see each other at dinner."

"Before you go," Daniel said, "let me check the corridor." He went to the door, glanced through the peephole then opened the door just a little so that he could look out. Finally, he held the door wide. "All clear."

Alex left the room and walked to the opposite end of the hallway. She descended the stairwell all the way to the first floor where the summit meetings were being held. The short visit with Daniel had managed to calm her. Somehow, she knew if she got in a pinch, he would help her out of it. She didn't know much else about him, but her instincts told her he was a good guy even if he wasn't telling her the whole truth about himself. What male escort was all that concerned about identifying potential assassins?

CHAPTER 7

As soon as Alex left his room, Striker went after her to make sure she made it back to the summit meetings safely.

She took the elevator down.

Striker took the stairs, with the intention of running all the way down the five flights of steps. When he reached the second floor, the stairwell door opened, and he almost ran into Alex as she pushed through.

She stopped, her eyes widening until she realized it was him. Her lips curved into a wide smile.

Striker's heart warmed. "You should smile more often."

Her smile faded. "You have to have something to smile about."

A grin spread across his face. "I guess that means seeing me made you smile."

Her lips twisted. "Seeing someone on the stairwell, who isn't the man in the black ski mask, is much more pleasing than running into him again."

"I'm still taking it as a compliment," he said.

Her brow wrinkled. "Are you headed for the summit meetings?" she asked.

"No," he said. "I was making sure you got there. I take it getting off on the second floor was another of your diversionary tactics."

She nodded.

He tipped his head toward the stairs. "I'll follow you down, but I won't step out with you."

She gave him a brief smile. "Thanks." Her eyes narrowed. "Why are you being nice to me?"

Striker chuckled. "To tell you the truth, I don't know." Charley had told him to keep an eye on her, but he didn't have to go to all the effort of letting her stay with him and share his bed. Something about her made him do things he'd never done before. "Maybe it's just that I like you."

Her frown deepened. "Why?"

He gripped her arms in a gentle hold. "You intrigue me, and I admire a woman who can look out for herself."

Alex cocked an eyebrow. "Then why are you following me around to make sure I get to the meetings all right?"

Striker grinned. "It's in my nature to protect."

He bent and pressed his lips to her forehead. "Go, or you'll be late."

She blinked up at him, her eyes wide. Then she turned, pushed through the door and bolted. It was almost as if she were running from him.

The door closed between them before Striker realized why she'd hurried away.

He'd kissed her.

What had he been thinking?

That was just it...he hadn't been thinking. Kissing her had felt as natural as breathing.

He waited until she was almost all the way across the grand lobby before he exited the stairwell.

The Energy Summit attendees were moving toward the conference room, some hurrying, others talking with their peers as they moved in the general direction.

"What does a male escort do with his time when he's not escorting?" a familiar voice said to him.

He turned to find Natalya, dressed in a calf-length red dress and black high heels. Her makeup was flawless, and her auburn hair was pulled up in a messy bun on the crown of her head. For a woman her age, she was stunning, confident and seemed to know just about everyone at the event.

"I find that people-watching entertains me," he said.

Natalya fell in step with him, slipping her hand

through the crook of his elbow. "Observing people is a good way to learn things about them that they don't necessarily want you to know."

Striker glanced down at the woman. "Like?"

"People are creatures of habit. You might find that they always have coffee at exactly seven o'clock in the morning. They might run the same route every morning, if they're into exercise. Some men like to use events like this to leave their wives behind and spend time with their girlfriends."

"Interesting," Striker commented. "And you've been to enough of these kinds of conferences to observe all that?"

She nodded. "Knowing the players in any event gives you an advantage."

"How does that help you as an interpreter?" he asked, his gaze meeting hers and holding.

Her lips curled upward on one corner. "Let's just say...knowledge is power." She gave him a broad smile, released his arm and took a step away. "Now, if you'll excuse me, I have a job to do."

He dipped his head and watched as she walked away with a firm, determined gait.

The woman was an enigma. Most interpreters faded into the background.

Not Natalya. She stood out like a cape in a bull-fighter's arena. It was almost like she owned the bull, or bulls, in this case.

Striker wondered what other activities she

participated in besides interpreting. If she was as observant as she seemed, she could be blackmailing diplomats and leaders from a variety of different countries.

She was one to watch.

"Striker?" Charley's voice sounded in his ear.

"Yes, ma'am."

"Are you some place where you can talk?" she asked.

"No, ma'am," he said and headed for the elevator. "Let me get to my room where I can speak freely."

"Good. I have some information about Ms. Sokolov that you might find interesting."

Striker's pulse kicked up. "Give me a couple minutes."

"I'll stand by."

He entered the elevator and, using Alex's method, punched the button for the fourth floor. Once the elevator opened, he headed for the stairs and climbed to his floor. When he was safely in his room, he closed the door and engaged the lock. "Okay. I'm in my room. Shoot."

"Boot your laptop," she ordered.

He crossed to the desk, opened the laptop and waited for the screen to come up. Moments later, an image of a family appeared in front of him. A man, a woman and a little girl with raven-black hair.

He immediately knew the girl was Alex. "Alex's family," he said softly.

"That's right," Charley said. "They went by the names Mischa and Pavel Federov and their daughter Anya."

"Not Alex Sokolov?"

"Not at the time that photo was taken." Charley paused. "Their real names were Inna and Petyr Sokolov. Their daughter Alexa probably never really lived with that name. She was very young when they moved to Russia and became the Federovs. You see, Inna and Petyr were CIA sleeper agents embedded in Moscow, working for members of the Russian government and passing secrets to their handlers in the CIA."

His breath held. "Did Alex know what they did?"

"That, I don't know," Charley said. "She lived with her parents until she was in her mid-twenties when Inna and Petyr were killed in a housefire. At least, that was how it was reported. The press assumed the entire family perished in the fire, including the couple's daughter. The fire was so hot, there wasn't much left of their remains."

"Alex escaped." Striker could imagine the horror she'd witnessed.

"And the Russians assumed she'd died along with Mischa and Pavel."

"Until now," he said.

"We captured an image of her face when you two were viewing the reception hall videos. Our facial recognition software went to work going through stored video images from all over the world. We found clips stored on the CIA's database. Apparently, the CIA has had sightings of her over the past two years. They want to bring her in for questioning about her parents' deaths, but every time they get close, she disappears. The night her parents were killed, the Federovs were supposed to meet with one of their handlers to hand over something important."

"The CIA told you that?" Striker asked.

Charley chuckled. "Let's just say I have ways to gather information. I suspect Alexa got out of the house and could have whatever her parents were supposed to pass to the CIA. Thus their interest in bringing her in for questioning."

Striker stiffened. "Someone broke into her room last night. Was it the CIA?"

"No, but there are agents at the Energy Summit watching. The night the Sokolovs were killed, they'd contacted their handler, stating they had information they needed to pass to the director of the CIA. The Sokolovs insisted on meeting in person to hand it over. They never made their scheduled drop.

"There's something else you should know concerning Alexa." Charley paused.

Striker tensed.

"The CIA isn't sure, but they think she might be the person responsible for the deaths of a number of men who've been linked to a team of mercenaries who were in Moscow the night her parents died. She might also be linked to the death of a member of the Russian government and an informant for the CIA. The Sokolovs worked with him. The CIA thinks that guy was a double agent, working both camps. He might have been the one who exposed the Sokolovs."

A mercenary team, a house fire and assassinations. Daniel shook his head. "It fits. She has some self-defense skills not usually taught in public schools."

"If she is responsible for the deaths of the mercenaries and the double agent, she could be highly dangerous. And she might be the one targeting the Russians."

"She didn't stab Anatoly," Striker said.

"Maybe not, but she could be working with someone else."

"If she was behind the assassinations of the mercenaries and the double agent, it appears she might be after those responsible for killing her parents. What do Anatoly Petrov and Sergei Baranovsky have in common with her parents or the people she has targeted?"

"Anatoly was the double agent's boss."

Alex had said she didn't want to kill Anatoly, that she needed him. "Is it possible Anatoly knows who might have put a hit out on her parents?"

"Anything's possible in the Russian government. Sometimes, it's a free for all with every man looking out for himself," Charley said. "Many of the key leaders are also involved with the mafia. My main concern is that you watch Ms. Sokolov but be careful. If she knows you're following her, she could become a threat."

Striker laughed. "I've been keeping a close eye on her. In fact, after the attack last night, I had her stay in my room."

A moment of silence followed, then Charley said, "I know. Just be careful. She's tougher than you might think. Especially if she was able to eliminate trained mercenaries. Do you have any questions?" she concluded.

"About a hundred," he said, "but all for Ms. Sokolov."

"It's up to you whether you want her to know that you're on to her."

"Thank you for the leeway to make that decision," he said.

"Keep me informed."

"Roger," Striker said.

"Out here," Charley said.

Striker pulled the earbuds out of his ears. His first instinct was to throw them across the room.

Alex? An assassin?

He'd known she was more than just an interpreter. But an assassin? He'd only been kidding
when he'd accused her of being one. Then again,
his gut might have been working harder than his
gray matter. With hours to kill until the summit
meetings adjourned for the evening meal, Striker
went online searching for anything about the
Federovs and the Sokolovs. It was as if their existence had been wiped clean from the web.

Charley had access to a lot more databases than
he did, and she had the people and knowledge to
find it. He still didn't know much about Charley
and what her ultimate goal was, but he had signed
on with her operation. He prayed she was one of
the good guys.

The hours passed slowly. He left his room to
find a hot cup of coffee and sat in the ornate lobby
of the Hotel Le Negresco, watching people as they
walked by. Occasionally, one of the summit attendees emerged from the conference to take a phone
call. They didn't stay long, returning to the discussion as quickly as possible.

When four o'clock finally rolled around, the
doors to the conference center opened, and people
flowed out, talking heatedly. Some went directly to
the elevators. Others stood in the lobby discussing
the day's topics in various languages.

When the German delegate emerged, Striker's

pulse quickened. Not long after, Alex walked out. Her gaze scanned the lobby until it landed on him. Her eyes widened, and a smile touched her lips. Then she looked away and headed for the elevator.

Striker took the stairs to the third floor, climbing them two at a time.

He eased open the stairwell door and spotted Alex heading toward him.

Once through the door, she stepped into his arms.

He automatically opened them and held her close, a hundred thoughts blazing through his head. Number one was the fact she'd walked straight into his embrace.

He should have been thinking about the possibility of her being an assassin, and that she'd killed a number of men.

But the scent of her hair and the way her body melted into his pushed all of that out of his mind for the brief moment she wrapped her arms around his waist.

Finally, she pulled back, her cheeks bright pink, her eyes wide. "I'm sorry. I must be tired."

"Come on." He took her hand and led her up the stairs to the fifth floor. He checked the hallway, waited for a man to enter his room, and then hurried her toward his.

Once inside, with the door closed behind them, Striker turned to face her.

"How was the meeting?" he asked when he really wanted to grill her on her real identity and ask her if she'd killed half a dozen men.

"Heated," she answered, slipping the jacket from her shoulders. "We need to get dressed for dinner. It starts in just a few minutes."

"We'll get dressed in a minute," he said. "What was that all about?"

She looked away. "What?"

"That hug in the stairwell."

She shrugged. "I told you...I'm tired. I don't know what came over me."

"It must take a lot out of you to interpret for politicians and government officials all day," he commented. "Is it harder than killing someone, Anya?" he said, using the name she'd gone by when she'd lived in Russia with her parents. He pinned her with his stare.

Alex's face paled. "I don't know what you're talking about."

"Anya Federov, daughter of Mischa and Pavel Federov, sleeper agents in Russia for the CIA." He cocked an eyebrow. "Does that ring a bell?"

She folded her jacket over her arm. "I don't—"

"You can cut the lies. I know who you are, and apparently, others do as well." He crossed his arms over his chest. "That had to be the reason someone attacked you last night. They know who you are. The question is, did they do it because you killed a buddy of theirs, or are they after something your parents might have given you before they died?"

She stood for long moment without speaking. The circles beneath her eyes seemed darker, the shadows in her eyes deepened.

"Look, Alex...or Anya...I don't know what your parents were up to or what they felt necessary to pass to the CIA. I don't care that you've killed bad guys. I've killed a few myself. I can't judge you on that basis. However, I do need to know what I'm up against. If I'm to protect you or help to keep the Russians alive to get this deal signed, I need to know who wants to kill who, and if you're going to slit my throat in the night."

"I would never slit your throat," she whispered, her eyes glistening with unshed tears. "I...I...hell. They know I didn't die in that fire." She looked up at him. "You know about the fire?"

He nodded.

"And my parents?" she asked, her voice catching on a sob. She swallowed hard. "They broke down our door, charged in with their machine guns and murdered my parents. I would've stayed and helped them, but I wasn't armed. My mother told me to go. She wanted me to take a flash drive from the safe and leave the house."

"They would've killed you if you'd stayed," Striker said.

Alex reached into her bra and removed a slim

flash drive. "I've held onto this for two years. I can't get into certain files because they're encrypted, and I've tried every combination of passwords I could imagine. I still don't know what that file contains or why my parents thought it was so important I needed to live to get it out of the house before they destroyed my home with my parents in it." A single tear slipped down her cheek. She brushed it away.

Striker's heart squeezed hard in his chest. He wanted to take her into his arms and hold her through her pain. "I don't know whether to believe you or to turn you over to the French police."

"Sometimes, I think it would be easier to turn myself over to the Russians and be done with it. Living a life of hiding and running is exhausting."

"So, you are Anya and Alexa?"

She nodded.

"Did you kill the mercenaries and the government official the CIA thinks you did?" he asked.

"The team of mercenaries were guns for hire," she said, her jaw hardening. "They'd kill anyone for a price."

"And the government official?"

She glanced away. "He was a family friend. I thought I could trust him to know I was still alive. I needed answers to questions about who killed my mother and father. We met by the river." She laughed. "He picked the location because he could easily dump me into the river and no one would know he was the killer. When he tried to push me in," she turned to face Striker, "I ducked and pushed him. The river was up from recent torrential rains. He was swept away, his body found days later. It was ruled an accident." Her lips twisted. "If I'd been the one to die in the river, it would have been the same. He was afraid I'd blow his cover, since he was my mother and father's CIA contact in Russia. I learned later that while he'd been passing information to the US, he'd also sold US secrets to the Russians. He was the one who told the Russians my parents had something they really needed, and that they were planning to pass it to the CIA."

"Was he the one who sent in the mercenaries?" Striker asked.

Alex shook her head. "No. He didn't have those kind of connections. He was a middle man, playing both sides for profit. Someone else sent the gunmen." Her eyes hardened. "I've been looking for the past two years for that person. At the same time, I've been trying to break the encryption on the flash drive with no success on either task."

"Why didn't you turn the flash drive over to the CIA?"

"I want to know what was so important my parents were willing to die for it. If I'd turned it over to the CIA, they wouldn't have told me, and they might have used the information for other than noble purposes. Bottom line is that I didn't trust them, or anyone else." She shrugged. "So, I kept it and stayed in hiding."

"Until now."

She nodded. "This was my best chance to find out who put the kill order out on my mother and father. Petrov was the next man in the food chain, and Baranovsky is just ambitious enough to have some influence and connections. They had to have been involved in some way. I only needed to get them alone to question them." She lifted her chin. "Then someone stopped me from doing that."

"My apologies." He pushed his hand through his hair. "The question is, what do I do with you now?"

She held out the flash drive. "If you have resources, you can help me determine what's on this device so I know what the motivation was for killing the people I loved."

He frowned. "You wouldn't give this to the CIA, but you're handing it over to me now?" Striker held up his hands. "You need to hang onto it. You don't know me from anyone. How do you know I haven't ingratiated myself with you to make you want to give me the information?"

"Because I'm tired. I figure you would've killed me if you'd wanted it that badly. Hell, you could've taken it off me while I slept and I'd never have known." She gave him a brief smile. "Which tells me you didn't know of its existence...until now."

"Still, it's yours. Your parents wanted you to

hold onto it and keep it safe. If you want to use my computer to try to access the files, you're more than welcome to try."

She snorted. "I've tried every combination of passwords my parents could've used. Nothing works."

"Maybe it's not about looking for passwords. Sometimes, people lock files with biometrics like fingerprints, retinal scans and facial recognition software."

"Then I'm really out of luck. My parents bodies burned in the housefire."

"There has to be a backdoor to get into the file," Striker said. "Have you worked with any hackers to see if they can get in?"

She nodded. "I've consulted several and followed their instructions. But I couldn't bring myself to hand over the flash drive to anyone else. If it was that important that it was worth killing people and burning a house to the ground, it could be something bad if it lands in the wrong hands."

Striker nodded.

Alex glanced at the clock on the nightstand. "Dinner is in a few minutes. If we don't show up, people will wonder why. And if I'm being watched, which I'm sure I am, they might come looking for me in your room since you're missing, too."

Striker's gut knotted. "I don't like the idea of you going down to dinner or even going back to the summit sessions. We don't know who is after you and when they will strike next."

"Yeah, well, we don't have much choice. I need to talk with Baranovsky and find out if he was the one to order the hit. I didn't come this far to leave emptyhanded."

"He's not going to admit to anything," Striker said.

"He might, with incentive." Alex pulled a knife out of her pocket and flipped it open. What had appeared to be a small pocket knife opened up into a lethal blade.

"Remind me to never make you mad," Striker said.

She lifted one eyebrow. "Don't kill anyone I love, and we're good." Alex moved past him into the room, rummaged through her backpack and pulled out a white dress. "I'll only be a minute in the bathroom." She took the dress and a small makeup kit into the bathroom and closed the door.

He still wasn't sure what to do with her, but he couldn't let her go back to her room, and he didn't feel comfortable letting her get another one, if one was even available, that could be broken into as easily. Hopefully, in a crowded banquet hall, she'd be all right. Then again, Anatoly Petrov had been attacked during the reception with people all around him.

Striker changed into one of the dark suits he'd

purchased with the money Charley had given him. When he was ready, he sat at the desk and brought up the computer. Alex had laid the flash drive on the desk before entering the bathroom. She really was giving him the opportunity to take it.

He wouldn't. But he would encourage her to keep trying to decrypt the security on the file she was attempting to get into.

A moment later, Alex emerged from the bathroom, her hair drawn back into a loose bun at the nape of her neck. The dress hugged her body like a second skin and flared out at her knees. With every step she took, the fabric swirled around her calves, drawing attention to her slim ankles and the silver sandals she wore. She'd applied a little makeup to her eyes, emphasizing their darkness, and lipstick on her lips.

She was stunning.

Striker's pulse ratcheted up.

She crossed the room, took the flash drive from the desk and tucked it into her bra. "Ready?"

He nodded, cursing himself for promising not to touch her.

Now that he knew who she was and some of the reasons she was in danger, he was glad she was staying with him. He'd better keep his promise and stay hands off. The woman was a skilled assassin.

CHAPTER 8

ALEX LEFT the room first and took the stairs to the third floor, and then crossed to the elevator, completing the descent to the ground floor. She crossed the beautiful circular lobby with its polished white columns and made her way to the banquet hall that had been decorated with shiny chandeliers and lovely flower arrangements and topiaries.

Natalya Zotin stood near Sergei Baranovsky and Hans Sutter. Thankfully, Alex wasn't required to provide translation services for the German during meals, unless he specifically requested her to do so. He hadn't. Alex suspected he found it a sign of weakness to rely on someone else to communicate his thoughts to others.

Wanting to avoid Natalya, Alex turned and made her way to a table with the Italian and French delegates. She knew just enough Italian to make light conversation and enough French to introduce herself. The evening meal went off without a hitch, the delegates having calmed down during the afternoon discussions. With Petrov indisposed, Baranovsky took control of answering any questions with regard to the pipeline.

During the course of the meal, Lorenzo Ricci, the Italian energy representative, and the French delegate, Gerald Bonhomme, got into a lively discussion of the day's topics, to include alternative energy sources, current energy sources, transit routes and joint ventures between the EU and Russia.

At one point, Ricci leaned over to Bonhomme and whispered in Italian, "I have heard that the Russians are shorting the EU millions of cubic feet of natural gas each year."

Alex didn't catch all the words, but she understood the context. Her ears perked, and she strained to hear the rest of the conversation while pretending to eat the boeuf Bourguignon on the plate in front of her. The meal was excellent, but she didn't have much of an appetite.

For the first time in two years, people around her knew who she was. She felt vulnerable, like she had a target pinned to her front and back. She stared around the room, searching for anyone staring back. The only gaze she met was Daniel's.

Now that he knew who she was and what she'd done, she was even more determined to learn more about him.

At the moment, the conversation next to her was interesting enough to capture her attention, and she focused on what they were saying while trying not to be too obvious.

"*Oui*," Bonhomme nodded. "I have heard the same. The Russians want us to pay for more gas than we are receiving.

The Italian nodded. "We need to address this in tomorrow's session. I will not agree to the new pipeline if we are being robbed."

Nothing had been said during that day's summit session along this topic. The men agreed to bring it up in the next day's meeting and changed the conversation to favorite vacation spots.

Alex tuned out for the remainder of the meal. When she could leave without being rude, she excused herself and left the banquet hall. Out of the corner of her eye, she saw Daniel push to his feet and take his leave of the people rising from his dinner table.

She was nervous about being alone with him in the room. Now that he knew everything, she had nothing to hide. All the Krav Maga training in the world didn't make her feel any less vulnerable because Daniel was different. He wasn't after her to kill her. He hadn't tried to take her flash drive, even when she'd left it in front of him while she'd gotten ready for dinner.

He'd been there when she'd needed help, letting her stay in his room when someone had broken into hers.

And he hadn't tried to take advantage of her sexually, like so many men had since she'd grown into her womanly shape.

She glanced around the banquet hall one more time, searching for those who might be watching her every move.

Baranovsky stood and held Natalya's chair as she rose from the table. He said something in her ear and stepped back. She glanced across the room, her gaze meeting Alex's. She raised a hand and waved.

Alex dipped her chin in acknowledgement.

Baranovsky looked up, his eyes narrowing to slits. He turned to Natalya and spoke, his expression intense, his lip curling back in a snarl.

Natalya responded, her lips tight. She hooked her hand through Baranovsky's arm and led him toward the exit. Alex waited until they disappeared through the door before she made her way out. Even then, she paused at the exit and scanned the corridor. When she didn't see Natalya or the Russians, she headed for the lobby and the bank of elevators.

She made it there without being waylaid by

anyone. Once in a car with other guests, she got off on the third floor, looked around, then headed for the opposite stairwell from the one she'd used earlier. Two flights later, she hurried down the fifth floor corridor to Daniel's door and raised her hand to knock.

He opened the door before she could tap it with her knuckles and stepped back to allow her to enter. "Any tails?"

She shook her head. "No. I had to wait for Natalya and Baranovsky to leave the banquet hall and give them time to get to the elevators before I could head that way."

"Well, you're here now. I'm going to jump in the shower," Daniel said.

"Could I use your computer?" she asked.

He nodded. "Of course." Daniel opened the laptop. The image of her as a child with her parents was still on the screen.

Alex froze, her gaze fixed on the monitor.

"You were a cute kid," Daniel said softly. "You look like your mother. She was a beautiful woman."

She reached out to touch the screen, her heart squeezing so hard it hurt. "I miss them." Alex looked to Daniel. "Where did you get the photo? I don't have anything from our lives together. It all burned to the ground with the house."

"My...friend found it online."

Alex turned to Daniel and frowned. "No way.

123

My parents never posted anything online. Try again."

"My friend has connections with a lot of government agencies and some not so reputable places," he said.

"Who are you, really?" she asked. "And don't tell me you're a male escort. You're not."

He sighed. "You're right. I'm not a male escort. However, I've learned that I could do the job if I need the money…and I have needed the money in the not so distant past."

She tapped her toe, impatiently.

He blew out a deep breath. "Okay. I'm Dane Ryan. I'm working for a woman I haven't met in person, only spoken to over the phone. She hired me because of my training."

Alex studied the man. Dane Ryan seemed to fit him better than Daniel Rayne. It was a strong name worthy of a strong man. She liked it…she liked him, even if he had lied about who he was. The fact was, she'd lied, too. "What kind of training?" she asked.

"I'm a former Navy SEAL." As he said the words, he stood taller and squared his shoulders. "Unfortunately, I was asked to leave because of a mission I performed based on orders from people in a higher paygrade than I was. Their bosses didn't like the results, so they made me the sacrificial lamb."

"What was the mission?" she asked.

"To take out a bad egg in Russia."

Her eyebrows rose. "Assassination?"

"I like to think of it as a termination. The man tortured a number of Americans before killing them."

"So they sent you as the judge, jury and executioner."

He nodded.

"And they kicked you out for following orders?"

Again, he nodded.

Alex shook her head. "I took out a few people who killed others." She looked away. "I didn't like what I did, but I couldn't let them do it to others. They did it for money. No emotions. No concern for anything but filling their bank accounts."

He nodded. "I did what I had to do for my country."

She lifted her chin. "I did what I had to do for my family. And I'm not done."

"I'm not actually certain what my role is here now. My original assignment was to stop an assassination of one or more of the Russian delegates to make certain the agreement for phase two of the Nord Stream pipeline goes through." His lips curled on the corners. "It seems I almost failed my first mission."

Her lips twisted. "Because Petrov was stabbed while you were dealing with me."

"Now it seems, my boss wants me to keep an eye on you. That you could be potentially more important than the Russians and the signing of the agreement."

Alex frowned. "Why does she think I'm more important?"

He tipped his head toward her chest.

Her eyes widened. "The flash drive?"

"Yes. It appears someone wants it. If it's important enough to kill for, they'll be back to take it from you. Have you made a copy of it?"

She shook her head. "I tried, but it wouldn't let me. I can't do anything with the file because of the encryption. My parents kept other information on that disk, like bank accounts and contact names, and I was able to get to those, but not that one file." She tilted her head to one side. "If my parents locked it with biometrics, is it possible to access it another way?"

"My new boss might have people who can crack the code. She said their intent was to turn it over to the CIA. Why not do that, now that you know that's what they wanted?"

"I should," Alex said. "I'm not getting anywhere on my own, and I don't want to use members of the dark web to accomplish the task. That's what bothers me—not knowing why the information is so important. I don't want any organization to have it if it will cause a world war or mass destruction."

"What if it's a cure for some horrible disease that the Russians have been holding out on?" Dane shook his head. "Think about it. I can get my boss to check with the CIA for a contact if you want to hand it off to them."

Alex didn't know what she wanted to do with the flash drive that she'd carried for the past two years. It was the last thing she possessed that had belonged to her parents, besides the passports that had been in the safe.

"You don't have to decide now." Dane took her hand in his and pulled her into his arms. "It's enough to think about for a while." He held her close without making her feel trapped. Instead, she felt warm, safe and...cherished. She hadn't felt any of those things since her parents had passed. She stood in the circle of his arms for a long moment, inhaling his scent and savoring his strength. On her own for two years, she hadn't had anyone she could lean on.

After a while, he tipped her chin up. "As much as I like holding you, I need a shower and we both need rest." He kissed her forehead like he had earlier that day.

Alex's pulse quickened. She lifted her chin and rose up on her toes, brushing his lips with hers. "Thank you."

He chuckled. "I've never had a woman thank me

for kissing her on her forehead. Other places, yes. But not on the forehead."

Her cheeks heated. "For making me feel safe."

He brushed a strand of her hair back behind her ear. "I'm here for you, and I want to help. I can't promise to help you kill the person who put the hit on your parents. But I'll do my best to keep you safe as long as I'm here."

She hugged him around his waist, and then stood back. "You'd better get that shower. I want one after you."

"You're welcome to go first," he said.

"No. I want to try one more time to get into that file. There has to be a password I haven't considered."

He waved a hand toward the laptop. "Have at it." Then he disappeared into the bathroom. Shortly after he left her, Alex could hear the sound of the shower turning on.

Alex closed her eyes and inhaled the lingering scent of his cologne. Her pulse still hammered through her veins, and warmth coiled low in her belly. Dane stirred something inside her she hadn't felt in a very long time.

Desire.

She drew in a deep breath, willing her heartbeat to return to normal. Why did the man have such a strong effect on her? They barely knew each other, and they would be parting ways once the Energy

Summit concluded. Unless she agreed to hand over the flash drive to the CIA. In that case, Dane might be her escort and protector until that task was complete. She might even insist they make the transfer in the States.

Whatever happened, her identity was known by someone who wanted something from her or wanted her dead before she could pass on the drive. For the past two years, she'd more or less played dead. Now that she was known to be alive and well, she was vulnerable.

Her first instinct was to disappear, fade into the dark and not come up until she knew for certain who had hired the mercenaries to kill her parents. She'd surface long enough to take him out, and then start over somewhere else.

Maybe she'd move to Montana or Colorado. Or live in an ex-pat community in Costa Rica or Guatemala. She'd dreamed of doing that once she'd completed her mission. She'd set up a house... alone. Before she'd met Dane, that dream had sounded idyllic.

Now? Not so much.

She'd put her life on hold, gotten blood on her hands and done things that would put her in jail in the States, if anyone could tie the actions back to her. She had no room in her life for anyone else. She'd have to be in hiding for a very long time no matter where she ended up.

A man like Dane would want to have the perfect home, wife and children. He was an honorable man who'd given his loyalty to his country.

And for what? To be kicked out of the career he'd trained so hard to master?

Alex shook the idea of a happily-ever-after with Dane from her thoughts. It would never happen. It couldn't.

She sat at the desk, inserted the flash drive into the side of the computer and clicked on the icon that popped up. As usual, she had no problem getting into the personal information her parents had stored there. The bank accounts they'd set up with cash she'd ultimately moved to other accounts on the Cayman Islands. The file she couldn't get to was labeled PAV. She'd thought for the longest that it was her father's name abbreviated. Now, she wasn't so sure.

When she clicked on the file she didn't get the usual error. The file didn't come up, but the computer's cursor spun as if working, churning on something. The built-in camera light flashed on then off.

Her pulse picked up. Was the computer safe to use? Did someone have remote access to it? Had they just taken her picture?

The churning cursor blinked out, disappearing from the screen.

Alex moved her finger across the touchpad, trying to find the cursor.

The screen filled with what appeared to be a document. The words on the page didn't make sense. Some were English, intermingled with letters and numbers.

The door to the bathroom opened behind her, and Dane walked out wearing shorts with a towel draped around his neck.

He crossed to where Alex sat in front of the laptop, her heart beating hard inside her chest.

"It opened," she whispered, the enormity of what had just happened threatening to overwhelm her.

"What's in it?" he asked, leaning over her shoulder.

"I'm not sure," she said.

He stared at the screen for a few moments. "It looks like some kind of computer programming language."

"That doesn't help me much."

"All the more reason to get it to someone who knows what it is," Dane said.

"I need to hand it over to the CIA." She looked up into Dane's eyes. "Do you trust this boss of yours?"

"So far, she seems to care about the fate of the world. I can ask her to get you to the States to hand it over to the folks at Langley in Virginia. They'll have the expertise to decipher the code. How did you get it to come up? Did you remember a password that worked?"

She shook her head. "I think the computer took my picture. The next thing I knew, the file opened."

Dane nodded. "Biometrics. I bet it used facial recognition. Your parents must have used a photo of you to lock the file. Only you could open it."

"Then I have to deliver this flash drive in person," she said. "Otherwise, they won't be able to access it or they'd have to spend a lot of time finding a workaround."

"If you're sure you want to hand it over, I'll get in touch with my boss and have her set up the transfer at Langley."

Alex stared at the gibberish on the screen. "This is what they wanted."

"Or wanted to keep anyone else from getting their hands on," Dane suggested.

She nodded. "I wonder what the code does."

"When you hand it over to the CIA, you might not ever know."

She sighed. "Unless I teach myself this computer language, I'll never know anyway." Alex squared her shoulders. "Set it up. I'll hand it over on one condition."

He frowned. "What condition?"

"That I'm allowed to go free."

"Why wouldn't you be allowed to go free?"

She turned toward him. "You and your boss know what I've done. In the States, that's considered murder."

"Only if someone presses charges. I doubt seriously anyone will press charges for the murder of mercenaries in a foreign country."

"Still, I want it in writing that they'll expunge my record. I don't want to have it hanging over my head for the rest of my life."

Dane nodded. "I'll let the boss know." He held out his hand. "Now, we need to get some sleep."

She closed the file, ejected the flash drive, carried it to the nightstand on her side of the bed and laid it on the wooden surface. "That little device got my parents killed." Alex climbed into the bed and lay back, staring at the ceiling.

"No," Dane said as he got in on the other side, "the person who wanted that device got your parents killed."

She turned to face him, moving the pillows aside. "Have you ever wanted a reset of your life? To take yourself back to a time when there seemed to be nothing wrong with your world?"

He gave half a smile. "Yes and no. Things happen for a reason. If I hadn't made my mark and been booted out of the Navy, I never would have met you."

"And if my parents hadn't been murdered, I don't know where I'd be now." She stared across at him. "I wouldn't be lying next to a stranger, wishing I had the nerve to kiss him."

He chuckled. "I promised I wouldn't touch you unless you wanted me to."

Her pulse raced through her veins, her blood getting hot and getting hotter. "You've already broken that promise twice by kissing me on my forehead."

"I have, but I won't go any further."

"Unless I want it," she concluded.

"Right."

She met his gaze. "I want it."

CHAPTER 9

His PULSE RACING, Striker stretched out across the bed, moved the barrier pillows, tossing them to the floor. "Are you sure?"

She nodded. "It's been a long time since someone held me close. I'd forgotten how good it feels."

He reached out and pulled her into his arms. "I can hold you, if that's all you want," he said, fitting her body against his.

She rested her head on his shoulder. "Let's start here," she murmured. "Like I said, it's been a long time."

Striker brushed a strand of hair back from her forehead. "You have the most beautiful hair of anyone I've ever known."

She smiled. "I got the thickness from my

mother and the color from my father. My mother had brown hair. My father had jet black."

He twirled a long strand around his finger. "Best of both," he concluded, "and so soft."

She tentatively laid a hand on his bare chest. Her fingers weren't cold like some of the women Striker had known. They were warm and strong, pressing into him, curling just a little until her nails scraped his skin.

He leaned closer and pressed another kiss to her forehead, wanting to claim her lips but—

Alex tipped her head just enough to capture the kiss meant for her forehead. "If you're going to kiss me, do it like this." She pressed her mouth against his and ran her tongue across the seam of his lips.

He opened to her, liking how she took charge. At least with her making all the moves, he'd know how far she wanted to go. So far, so good. And he had a condom in his wallet on the nightstand should they take it all the way.

The hand on his chest moved, skimming over his muscles and down his torso.

Blood thrummed through his veins, pushing heat lower. His groin tightened, and his cock thickened, pressing into her thigh. He prayed she didn't stop. There was so much more of this woman he wanted to know.

Every last inch.

Her tongue slid past his teeth and caressed his

in a long, slow glide, sending his body into a tail-spin of longing.

He cupped her cheek in the palm of his hand and deepened the kiss, hungrily consuming her mouth until they both broke away to catch their breath.

She tasted good, the mint of her toothpaste lingering in his mouth, the touch of her hand moving down his torso stirring him into a hard, urgent knot. If she backed down now, how would he have the self-control to stop? He wanted all of her.

When her fingers reached the elastic of his shorts, he drew in a sharp breath and let it out slowly. "Don't go there if you don't want what comes next," he warned. "I pride myself on my self-control but, woman, you're making me lose it fast."

She chuckled and looked up into his eyes as she slid her hand beneath the elastic and encircled his dick with her fingers. "I'm not afraid," she said. "I know what I'm doing." Her gaze held his. "Do you?"

He cupped her hand through the fabric of his shorts. "Yes."

She ran her hand up and down his shaft, her warmth and gentleness making him harder by the second. Finally, he had to remove her hand so that he could shed his shorts. Then he rolled her onto her back and leaned his body over hers. "Now would be the time to tell me you want me to stop."

"I don't want you to stop," she said and leaned her head up to brush her lips over his. "I want everything you've got." She grabbed the hem of her shirt and started to drag it up her body.

Striker brushed her hands aside, leaned back, straddling her hips, and pulled the shirt over her head. He tossed it onto a chair beside the bed and bent to take her lips with his in a blood-burning kiss that took his breath away.

He broke away long enough to suck air into his lungs and then seared a path of kisses and nibbles along the side of her neck down to where the pulse thrummed against the base of her throat. Based on how fast her heart was beating, she was as excited as he was. But he wanted her even more so before he quenched his thirst for this woman.

Moving slowly down her body, he kissed and flicked her skin with his tongue until he reached her breasts. There, he captured one of her rosy nipples in his mouth and sucked gently until the tip hardened into a bead. Moving to the other breast, he rolled the tip between his teeth and flicked it with his tongue.

Alex writhed beneath him, her hips rising, her hands running over his back, her nails scraping his skin. She threw back her head and moaned softly.

Striker took that as a challenge. He wanted her so bothered she called out his name. Moving lower, he flicked his tongue across her ribs, and downward, until he came to the thin elastic of her panties. He hooked his fingers into the band and dragged the undergarment down her legs and past her ankles, finally tossing them over his shoulder.

He lay down between her legs, parted her folds and slid a finger into her slick, wet channel.

Alex's knees drew up, and she dug her heels into the mattress, her hips rising.

Striker added another finger and another, then lowered his mouth to claim that little nubbin of flesh of tightly packed nerves. He sucked on it gently then flicked his tongue across the velvety smoothness.

Alex moaned and raised her hips, urging him to continue.

He did, stroking her there with his tongue, his fingers swirling in a tight pattern.

Alex's body tensed beneath him. In the next moment, she let go, riding her release for the next few minutes, her hips rocking and her fingers digging into the comforter.

When she finally lay back against the mattress, he climbed up her body and reached over her to snag his wallet from the nightstand. He extracted a condom and handed it to her.

"How thoughtful," she said and took the offering. "I'm glad someone is thinking straight," she murmured.

"Always come prepared," he said and kissed her full on the lips.

Alex tore open the packet and slid the condom over his thick staff. When she was done, she wrapped her hands around the base and fondled his balls.

Striker sucked in a breath and held it, while a wave of sensations washed over him.

Her hand guided him to her entrance and urged him to dive in.

He paused at her opening, dipping in slowly to lubricate his cock as he pressed ever deeper into her.

She was tight.

He was big, and didn't want to hurt her.

Alex gripped his hips and slammed him home.

He drove all the way inside her and held steady, allowing her to adjust to his length and girth. When he thought she'd had enough time to get used to him inside her, he moved, pumping in and out. Slowly at first, and then faster, until he was thrusting in and out at a swift pace.

Alex raised her knees and dug her feet into the mattress so that she could raise her hips and meet him thrust for thrust.

He moved like a piston, in and out, until the tension inside him grew to a fevered frenzy, and he thrust on last time. The sensations rocketing through him shot him over the edge. His cock throbbed deep inside Alex.

When he was spent, he rolled her and him onto their sides and settled beside her.

She rubbed her hand over his chest. "Is it always like this?" she whispered.

"Like what?" he asked. "Too fast and not enough foreplay? Was the dismount too soon?"

Alex laughed. "No. None of those. Is it always this amazing?"

He shook his head. "Sometimes, it's even more amazing."

"I'm not sure I believe you. That was pretty... good." She pressed a kiss to his chest and looked into his eyes. "Show me how much better it can be."

He laughed out loud. "Give me a minute to recover from that round."

Her brow wrinkled. "Hurry it up. I'm so hot, I can hardly stand it. I need more of what you have to offer." She fondled his balls again. "This is where we started. Show me some more of that magic."

He groaned, rolled back up onto his hands then leaned forward and kissed her lips. He slid his still thick and hard shaft into Alex's depths and started all over, showing her just how much more amazing making love could be.

When they finally fell back to the mattress, he gathered her in his arms and fell asleep with her pressed up against him. Life didn't get better than this. He loved what had just happened between them, and he wanted so much more.

Two days with Alex wasn't nearly enough. Somehow, he had to make their time together last longer than the two days of the summit.

He wasn't ready for this, whatever it was, to end.

ALEX LAY FOR A LONG TIME, inhaling the scent of Striker, committing everything about him to her memory. When the summit ended, she wouldn't see the handsome SEAL again. They weren't meant to be together. Alex didn't believe there was anybody out there who was meant to be with her. She was a cold-blooded killer who'd taken matters into her own hands to find and punish those who'd taken the lives of her mother and father. Who could love that kind of person?

She pressed her ear to his chest, listened to the steady beat of his heart and imagined a world where she wasn't running from Russians wanting to kill her. And there was still the matter of finding the person who'd sent the kill order for her family.

Alex sighed and snuggled closer, embracing the man and the moment that couldn't last more than a night. Finally, she slept off and on, waking before the warm light of day.

While Striker continued to sleep, she slid out of

the bed and into the bathroom for a shower before the start of another day of interpreting and praying whoever was after her didn't make a move during the summit. She needed to find time to question Baranovsky about his connection with Pavel and Mischa Federov.

The summit had been an ideal opportunity to get the two men alone. In Russia, Alex didn't know who to be wary of. Anyone on the streets of Moscow could recognize her as her mother's daughter. In France, only the few Russians had a chance of knowing who she might be.

Alex turned on the water, waited for it to warm and stepped beneath the spray. Water ran over her face and down her body, following the same path Striker's mouth had blazed the night before. Her core heated at the memory.

Warm, strong hands slid around her waist and pulled her against a rock-solid body. The evidence of desire nudged her buttocks, sending ripples of electricity through her.

Alex leaned back and tipped her head to the side, allowing Striker to skim his lips across the back of her ear and neck. "I have to be downstairs soon."

"I know," he said and kissed the curve of her neck. "I couldn't resist."

She turned in his arms, cupped his cheeks in her

palms and leaned up on her toes to brush his lips with hers.

He tightened his arms around her back and crushed her mouth, claiming her tongue in a sensual dance.

Her blood humming through her veins, Alex melted into Striker. She couldn't get close enough.

Striker's hand slipped between them and cupped her sex. One finger found its way into her, and then another, while his thumb strummed her clit.

She had a difficult time dragging air into her lungs.

Then he stopped and leaned back. Holding up a small packet, he cocked an eyebrow. "Yes or no?"

With her breath already labored, she managed to say, "Yes!" in a strangled whisper.

He handed her the packet.

Alex tore it open and rolled the condom over his engorged cock, amazed at how hard and thick he was and anxious for him to be inside her.

Striker scooped her up by the backs of her thighs and pressed her against the cool tiles of the shower wall. He bent to nuzzle her earlobe as he lowered her over him.

He slid into her slowly.

She was ready, her channel slick and clenching around him. Planting her hands on his shoulders and wrapping her legs around his waist, she rose up to the tip of his shaft then sank down again, loving how he filled her, stretching her to fit.

As their pace increased, he pressed her against the wall and held her there, thrusting again and again.

Alex forgot how to breathe as she shot over the edge, her body pulsing with her release.

Striker thrust one last time, sinking deep. His muscles remained tense as he rode his climax to the very end. When he finally drew in a deep breath and let it out, he lifted her off his shaft and set her on her feet. He peeled the condom off then he held her close, letting the water rush over both of them.

Alex could have stood there until her skin pruned. There was no other place she'd rather be than in his arms. She could get used to waking up to this every morning.

Unfortunately, there was an ugly world out there. Striker had just reminded her how beautiful it could be. Too bad what they were discovering in each other wouldn't last.

Striker squirted soap into the palms of his hands and rubbed them together creating a thick lather. He ran his hands all over her body, slowing at her breasts to tweak the tips of her nipples. Then he trailed his hand over her belly and down to cup her sex.

Alex did the same for him, her hands gliding

over his broad shoulders and down his tight abs to his cock, which jutted out, hard and velvety.

He sucked in a breath. "Keep that up and you won't get to the meeting on time."

She circled his shaft with her fingers and stroked him several times before she sighed. "If only we had the day to ourselves."

He maneuvered her around so that she stood beneath the showerhead and let the spray rinse the suds from her body.

Then he stepped beneath the spray, rinsed quickly and turned off the water.

Alex loved looking at his body. His muscles were tight, not a spare ounce of flesh anywhere.

They grabbed towels, dried each other off then dressed quickly.

"I'll have to hurry to get down to the banquet hall to snag a cup of coffee," she said.

"I'm ready," Striker said. "I'll follow you down the stairs."

She nodded, tucked the flash drive into her bra and headed for the door.

"Let me." Striker poked his head out the door, and then opened it wide. "All clear."

Alex led the way to the stairwell and hurried down the steps to the first floor. Before he exited, she turned to Striker, leaned up on her toes and pressed a kiss to his lips. "Thank you for reminding me what life is worth living for."

He frowned. "You're not going anywhere yet."

"This is the last day of the summit. Most people will leave at its conclusion," she said.

"You left your backpack in my room," he said.

Alex nodded. "I'll collect it later." She turned to leave, but he caught her hand before she could push the door open.

Striker spun her around and into his arms. "I'm not ready to end this...whatever this is between us."

"What else can we do? You have your work. I have mine."

"This can't be over when it's just begun." He crushed her mouth with his in a kiss that set her soul on fire. When he finally lifted his head, she was breathless.

He brushed a loose strand of her hair back behind her ear. "We'll talk later."

Alex nodded, turned and left the stairwell, tears welling in her eyes. How she wished she could have a normal existence where she could stop running and be with someone like Striker.

Impossible.

She was an assassin. He was a security guy. It would never work. She was destined to live a life alone for the safety of herself and anyone else she might fall in love with.

Her heart skipped several beats.

In love?

She wasn't in love with the Navy SEAL. Love

grew over time. They barely knew each other, having spent just a day and a half together. Sure, the sex had been out of this world, but that didn't make it love. Lust, yes. Love, no.

She entered the conference room and took her seat beside Hans Sutter. As usual, he didn't speak to her or acknowledge her existence.

Alex didn't mind. She'd rather have the quiet to study the people settling into their positions around the room.

The moderator kicked off the session introducing the Italian delegate.

Lorenzo Ricci stood and faced the other delegates. In Italian, he said, "Esteemed members of this summit, it has been rumored that the EU is not receiving all the natural gas they are paying for. Could someone please address this concern? Are we in fact paying for gas that is being siphoned off at or before it arrives at the Greifswald transfer station?"

As translators relayed the message, a rumble of anger sounded from the delegates around the room.

Hans smacked his palm against the table. In German, he said, "I, too, have heard such a rumor. I've had my scientists checking into usage and billing. The numbers don't add up. Explain."

A rumble of anger circulated through the room.

Baranovsky stood, his face ruddy red. In Russian, he practically shouted, "We do not steal from the EU. Who spreads such lies?" He stared around the room, a vein popping out on his forehead. "I will have words with this person."

The moderator did his best to bring the meeting back to order. The rest of the morning went no better. The members of the summit wanted to know more about the diverting of natural gas from the European countries.

Nearing lunch, Sutter had had enough. "Why should we approve of another pipeline when the one we have isn't delivering what we contracted? I've heard enough. I will cast my vote now."

The room exploded in loud conversations and shouting. The moderator banged a gavel several times to bring the room to order. He asked everyone to take time to think about it over lunch.

Eager to see Striker, Alex gathered her notes and stood. If this was the last day they might have together, she didn't want to miss a second.

Alex had just turned toward the door when a security guard burst through the door and shouted in French, "There's been a bomb threat. Everybody needs to move toward the closest exits now."

The delegates and their assistants started toward the security guard.

The man held up his hands. "The closest way out of the building is through the other end of this room. Follow the exit signs. Move quickly, but don't panic. It could be a hoax, but we don't want to ignore the threat."

Alex got caught up in the rush for the rear exits. She didn't want to go that way. If there was a real bomb threat, Striker needed to know. He could be in his room and not have heard the order to evacuate the building. Like swimming upstream, she pushed her way through the worried delegates moving in the opposite direction. When she finally made it past the last ones, she ran into a security guard and a member of the hotel staff.

The staff member blocked her path. "Madam, you must leave the building at once."

"I will, as soon as I know my partner is safe. He's up in his room." She tried to duck past the two, but they weren't budging.

"Tell me your room number, and I'll send someone up to make sure he gets out."

"I can do it myself, if you'll let me by," Alex said, ready to take the woman and the security guard down if she had to.

Another security guard joined them and asked why the guest had not vacated the premises.

The staff member frowned. "She refuses to go."

"Madam, if you do not leave on your own, we will be forced to escort you out." The new security guard reached for her arm.

For a moment, she considered fighting her way through, but Alex didn't want to start a ruckus, drawing attention to herself. She'd have to leave and come back in another way. "I'm going." She turned and left through the exit door at the rear of the conference room. The door led down a short hallway to a loading dock where a truck stood empty at the ramp. The last of the delegates were being herded down steps and around the other side of the building. Alex glanced around, searching for another door into the building. She tried one marked "receiving" in French. The door was locked. A button on the wall had a sign to ring the bell for assistance. When Alex moved past the truck, two men stepped out of the back. Both wore dark overalls like delivery truck drivers and had baseball caps pulled down low over their foreheads, shadowing their faces.

As gooseflesh rose on her arms, Alex moved past them quickly, heading for the steps leading down from the ramp. If she hurried, she might catch up with the other summit attendees.

The two men didn't give her the time she needed to reach the steps. They rushed toward her.

Alex ran, but she didn't reach the steps before one of the men reached out and grabbed her arm, spinning her on her heels.

She came around fighting, sending sidekick to his kidney.

The other man grabbed her other arm and shoved it up the middle of her back.

Pain shot through her arm, and she stood as high as she could on her toes to find some relief.

The one she'd kicked pulled something out of his pocket. It looked like a syringe.

Alex stomped on the instep of the man trying to break her arm.

He cursed and loosened his grip just enough Alex could pull her arm free and jab him with her elbow in the belly. She took two steps in her break-away and was yanked up short when the man with the syringe grabbed a handful of her hair and dragged her backward against him. Before she could regain her balance, he jabbed the needle into her arm.

He let go of her hair.

When Alex darted away, her legs turned to jelly, her vision blurred, and she crashed to the concrete.

CHAPTER 10

AFTER STRIKER SAW Alex to the summit session, he grabbed a cup of coffee and headed back to his room where he powered on the computer and fit his comm devices into his ears. He'd forgotten them earlier when he'd stepped into the shower with Alex.

"Striker," Charley's voice sounded in his ear.

"Yes, ma'am."

"I take it you revealed what you know about Ms. Sokolov?"

"I did."

"How did she respond?"

"Well," he said, "she said she'd been holding onto the flash drive since her parents' deaths because she wanted to know what was on it. For the past two years, she couldn't access one file on the drive. Everything else had to do with personal bank accounts and contacts. The file she couldn't open was encrypted."

"The CIA has entire teams devoted to decryption."

"I know that. She was worried that once she handed it over, she'd never learn what was actually on the file, what got her parents killed."

"That's quite possible," Charley agreed.

"Last night, she asked to use the laptop you assigned to me. While I was in the shower, she managed to get into that file. The laptop used the embedded facial recognition software, and it let her in."

"What did she find?"

"Programming code. Some kind of software."

"Interesting," Charley said.

"She doesn't know what the code means and doesn't want to learn how to read the language. She's ready to hand it off to the people her parents had intended it should go to. Do you have contacts at the CIA?"

"I do."

"Alex would like to meet personally with a representative of the CIA...at Langley. They will need her biometrics to get into the file."

"I can make that happen," Charley said. "When?"

"As soon as you can set it up."

"I'll get right on it. In the meantime, is she safe?"

"She's in the Energy Summit meeting surrounded by delegates from all over. I imagine the security is pretty tight. I'm about to head down to her."

"Good. Safeguard her and that flash drive. We can only imagine what's so highly important in that code."

"I'm on my way back down. They should be breaking for lunch soon." He paused. "Charley?"

"Yes, Striker?"

"My original assignment was to protect the Russians. Am I still working that mission?"

"I've been following the summit meetings," Charley said. "They're not going well, and probably will continue to be contentious. I'm more worried about what's in that software that has so many upset and eager to get to Alex to take it from her, or let it die with her. Stick with Alex. She's your number one priority for now."

"Good. I'm on it." He ended the call and hurried out to the elevator, taking it down to the first floor. When he stepped out of the elevator he saw security guards rushing across the huge lobby, urging people to leave through the exit doors. Members of the staff and security guards ran toward the conference rooms.

Striker ran with them until one of the hotel staff members turned to see him and said something in French.

"I don't speak French," Striker said without slowing.

The man caught his arm. "Monsieur, you must leave the hotel. There has been a bomb threat."

Striker shook off the man's hand. "My fiancée is in the Energy Summit. I'm not leaving without her." By then, they had reached the room in which the meetings had taken place.

A security guard emerged from the conference room.

When Striker tried to move past him, he stuck out an arm and rattled off something in French.

"Damn it, I don't speak French."

The guard switched to English. "The room is empty. The delegates left through the rear exit. They have been moved across the street, away from Hotel Le Negresco. If you're looking for someone, look there. Now, please, leave the building."

Striker pushed past him and ran across the large conference room to the rear exit and down a short corridor to a loading dock.

A truck was just pulling out of the ramp. No one else could be seen.

Striker ran down the steps and across the street to where a large group of men and women stood staring back at Hotel Le Negresco.

He found the German quickly and hurried toward him. "Do you speak English?" he asked.

The man nodded. "*Ja.*"

"Your interpreter...where is she?"

The man shrugged and glanced around. "She was moving into the hotel when everyone else was leaving. I do not know where she is now."

For the next couple of minutes, Striker wove through the people standing on the sidewalk waiting to hear the all-clear announcement so that they could return to their discussions. All the while, they were missing one of the attendees. He searched for Baranovsky, knowing Alex would take any opportunity to get him alone to find out if he was the one who'd put the hit out on her parents.

Baranovsky was missing from the crowd of delegates, and so was Natalya Zotin.

Striker's gut knotted. He had a bad feeling about this and wished he had equipped Alex with some kind of communications device. He needed help finding her.

He touched the earbud in his ear. "Charley, if you're listening, I could use a little help, here."

"I'm here," she said.

"Alex is missing."

"I know."

"How the hell do you know already when I just figured it out?" Worry sparked irritation. His boss seemed to know everything. It was creepy but might prove useful if she could help him find Alex.

"I had one of my people drop a tracking disc in her pocket. She left the hotel a few minutes ago.

She was traveling too fast to be on foot. We're tracking her but don't know exactly where she's headed. I've sent a driver to pick you up two blocks east of your hotel. He'll be there in three minutes. We'll feed him directions to where Alex is heading. You have three minutes. Go."

Striker ran out to the street and turned east. He sprinted the two blocks, arriving just as a black SUV pulled up to the curb. He jumped into the front passenger seat and turned to the driver. "Who sent you?"

"Charley," he answered as he drove east. He adjusted the volume on a radio affixed to the dash. A male voice gave him directions to follow the *Prom. Des Anglais,* the main road following the coast line. "She could be headed for the airport."

Why would Alex be going to the airport? Had she found the information she'd been after? Was she going back to Russia to finish what she'd started? If so, why hadn't she come back to his room to get her backpack first—and to say goodbye to him?

His chest was tight, and his pulse thrummed through his veins. She'd left without saying goodbye.

"She's at the airport," the voice said on the radio. "What's your ETA?"

"Fifteen minutes in this traffic," the driver replied.

"Make it sooner."

They were approaching a traffic light that was turning red.

The driver slammed his foot on the accelerator and swerved around a vehicle stopping at the light and swerved again to miss the little black sports car pulling through the green light on his side.

Striker braced for impact, sure the sports car was going to T-bone his side of the SUV. The sports car's driver slammed on his brakes and slid sideways, barely missing the SUV.

Striker's driver didn't blink an eye. He zigzagged through traffic, blowing through stoplights and scaring the shit out of Striker. He'd rather have been the one doing the driving. Then he would know what to expect and go even faster.

"Striker, she's on the taxiway." Charley said into his ear. "She must be in an airplane, waiting to take off."

Striker leaned forward as if it would get them there sooner. "Can't you get the ATC to stop the plane?"

"We're working on identifying the tail number," Charley said. "We can't stop the plane without cause."

"What if she's being kidnapped?" Saying the words made it all the more disturbing. "The bomb threat could have been a diversion to get her out of the building."

"We thought of that. But we can't be certain." Charley said something to someone in the background. "Striker, we've chartered a plane, and it's scheduled to take off in twenty minutes."

Striker clenched his fists. "Twenty minutes is twenty minutes too late."

"She has the tracking device on her still. We can follow her. Get to the airport. We'll find her."

"Just stop the damned plane."

"It's too late," Charley said. "It left the ground."

A SPLITTING HEADACHE WOKE ALEX. She hadn't felt this kind of pain since she'd had too much vodka with her friends at a nightclub in Moscow. The trouble was she couldn't remember drinking anything. She couldn't remember what she'd been doing to cause so much pain.

The last thing she did remember was...the summit...leaving the hotel through a rear door...a bomb threat.

She blinked her eyes open and frowned. This wasn't her hotel room, and it wasn't Daniel's.

No, Daniel wasn't right...

Dane. But he liked to be called Striker. Why was her head so fuzzy, and what was that roaring noise?

The room she was in dipped. She tried to put her arms out to steady herself only to discover she couldn't move them. Alex looked down at the duct tape wrapped around her wrists. She tried to move her legs but couldn't. They were bound at the ankles.

Then it all came back to her.

The bomb threat. The truck. The men in coveralls, wearing baseball caps, who'd grabbed her.

Her heart pounded against her chest as she stared around at the walls surrounding her. They weren't like normal walls, and she was in a small space with small round windows, lying across a couple of seats. And that roar like jet engines...

She was in an airplane.

Alex raised her bound hands to her right breast where she always tucked the flash drive in her bra. Her breath caught in her throat, and she almost moaned out loud.

It was gone.

The thunk of something dropping below her and snapping in place indicated landing gear had been deployed. But where were they landing? And who had taken her?

She struggled to sit up only to fall back onto the seat as the plane landed hard on the tarmac and screamed to a stop.

Two men appeared above her, grabbed her beneath her arms and hauled her to her feet.

"Who are you?" she demanded. "Where are you taking me?"

One of them tore a length of duct tape from a

roll and slapped it over her mouth. The other man dragged a cloth sack over her head and body, and then lifted her up, slinging her over his shoulder.

She bounced along, the man's shoulder digging into her belly as he descended the stairs out of the plane and walked across a hard surface. When he stopped, he dropped her onto another hard surface that smelled of rubber and oil. Then something slammed over her, taking away what little light had made it through the thick canvas of the sack that had been thrown over her.

An engine started. Not the roaring engine of a jet airplane, but a smaller one, like that of a car. Soon, they were moving along what sounded like paved roads with the occasional pothole.

Alex figured she was in the trunk of a vehicle.

She wiggled and scooted, trying to work the bag off her body. After several failed attempts, she finally managed to push it up over her head. Still trapped in a dark, confined space, she had only herself to get her out of this mess. Striker wouldn't have any idea where they'd taken her. He might even think she'd taken the opportunity to leave the summit and go back into hiding. She wondered if he'd be sad that she hadn't come to say goodbye.

Her heart ached at the thought of never seeing him again. He'd been the only person in a long time that she'd wanted to be around. And making love...

How would she survive without knowing that

feeling again? For that matter, how would she survive if she didn't find a way to free herself soon?

She felt around the interior of the trunk, searching for a rough edge to scrape the duct tape off her wrists. Every edge was smooth and of no use. With no other way to work through the tape, she tore into it with her teeth, working as quickly as she could. She had no idea how long they'd keep her in the trunk or where they were going.

Just as she tore through the last stretch of duct tape, the vehicle slowed to a halt. Muffled voices sounded outside. Alex strained to hear them. She only caught a few words, but it was enough to know they were speaking German.

They were being questioned by someone who was manning a gate. A moment later, she heard the clink of metal and something moving.

Alex reached for the tape at her ankles and tore at it with her fingernails, searching for the end so that she could unwind it.

Then the vehicle lurched forward and drove at a sedate pace for a short distance, eventually coming to a complete halt. The engine was shut off, and car doors opened and closed. Footsteps sounded around the side of the vehicle coming to a stop behind the trunk.

Alex hadn't succeeded in getting the tape off her ankles. She wouldn't get far if she attempted to make an attempt at escape. To keep her captors from discovering that she'd freed her wrists, she pulled the canvas sack over her head and lay still.

Just as she settled against the bed of the trunk, the lid opened and cool air wafted in. They weren't in Nice anymore.

Alex shivered. Wherever they'd taken her was much colder. She was almost thankful for the bag since she didn't have a coat to keep her warm.

Strong arms scooped her out of the trunk and flipped her onto a massive shoulder. She was carried into a building. They seemed to walk for a long time before they came to a stop. She heard the sound of a metal gate or door sliding open.

The man carrying her stepped forward. They sank a tiny bit, enough to let her know he'd carried her into an elevator.

The metal door closed, and the car went down at least one level before settling.

Alex was carried out of the elevator and dropped to the ground.

She landed hard on her hip and rolled to her side.

The sack was ripped off her head, and she blinked up at lights hanging over head. She held her hands together so that her captors wouldn't know she'd broken her bonds.

She'd been brought to what appeared to be some kind of control room with an array of monitors on one wall. The monitors were all blue screens with nothing else on them.

Men sat at keyboards keying frenetically, shaking their heads.

"Anya Federov," a familiar voice spoke from behind her. "Or should I call you Alexa Sokolov? What name are you most comfortable with?"

Alex rolled over and sat up.

Sergei Baranovsky stood with his arms crossed over his chest, his lip curled up on one side.

"Where are we?" Alex asked in Russian.

"You are at one of the Nord Stream substations, which is currently under attack due to ransomware."

"Why have you brought me here?" She reached down to pull the tape from around her ankles. It took her a moment to find the end and unwind the rest.

Baranovsky held up a small object.

Alex's heart sank into her belly. He had the flashdrive. For two years, she'd kept its secrets safe. Just when she'd planned on turning it over to the CIA, Baranovsky had come along and taken it before she could deliver it.

She tipped her head toward the device. "What do you think is on that flash drive, Sergei?"

"A way to keep from being crippled by vicious ransomware."

Alex raised her eyebrows. "The pipeline has been hit?"

"Yes. Two hours ago."

"I thought you had software to protect the pipeline from cyber-attacks," Alex said.

"I do, but my source is withholding delivery."

"Why?"

"For a bigger payoff."

"How many cubic feet are you losing every minute?" Alex asked.

"Too many. I must get the software that runs the distribution back online, immediately."

Alex shook her head. "Or you'll be found out for the fraud you are?"

"He will have more to lose than his dignity," a female voice sounded from across the room.

Natalya Zotin emerged from the shadows, wearing the royal purple dress she'd worn to the summit meeting earlier.

Baranovsky's face blanched. "How…?"

"How did I get here before you?" She laughed. "You forget, I have my own jet. I can go anywhere in the world whenever I want. Faster than anything you can charter with government money. I knew where you'd go as soon as the grid went down. All you had to do was give me a percentage of what you're siphoning off and none of this would have happened. The delegates would have eventually signed off on the Nord Stream two project and you'd have made even more money while keeping the gas flowing, both to the EU, and to me, because I hold the key to the ransomware."

Alex glanced from Natalya to Baranovsky, sick that she hadn't seen through Natalya's façade. "So, Sergei is stealing gas, and you want in on it?"

Natalya snorted. "He's not stealing anything right now. No one is getting natural gas out of this substation until the ransom is paid. And the ransom is fifty percent of what Sergei skims off the top and half of what he's put back in his Swiss bank accounts."

Sergei's eyes narrowed. "I don't need you or your key to the ransomware." He held up his hand. "I have the key."

Natalya's eyes flared so briefly Alex almost didn't catch the movement. Then she laughed. "You have nothing. My people have changed the parameters since the Federovs pirated a copy of my software. You have nothing."

"We'll see about that."

Natalya's glance went to Alex, and her lip curled up in a sneer. "You have the old software. Why did you bother to bring the Federovs' daughter here?"

"I might still have use of her. I understand the Federovs were keen on using biometrics. If they have any security in place, I might need the girl."

"I should have supervised the burning of the

house myself. Everyone and everything was supposed to burn to the ground."

Alex's face heated with the anger burning deep inside as the final key to her mother and father's murders became clear. "You were the one who ordered my home to be destroyed with my mother and father inside," she stated.

"They trespassed on my system and stole something that belonged to me. I made them pay for their transgression." The woman stood taller, her chin lifted high. "You were supposed to die with them, along with the pirated copy of software I paid for."

Alex drew in a deep breath, let it out and then lunged for Natalya, her claws out. This was the person who'd pulled the trigger on her parents. And she seemed proud of the murders she'd orchestrated.

Alex almost reached Natalya when two men stepped out from behind the woman and grabbed Alex's arms.

She fought them, kicking them in the shins and groin, but they didn't let go, stubbornly maintaining their grip on her arms.

"You killed my parents," Alex said through gritted teeth. "I will avenge them."

Natalya raised her arm. In her hand, she held a .40 caliber pistol, and she aimed it at Alex's face. "Not if you're dead."

CHAPTER 11

WHEN THE PLANE landed at the airport near Greifs-wald, Germany, Striker could barely wait for the steps to be lowered before he leaped to the ground.

Charley had said she'd send a car to pick him up and take him to where Alex's tracking device had stopped. The only vehicle waiting for him on the tarmac was a sleek black Ferrari sports car. As he ran toward it, Charley filled him in via the communications headset.

"It appears she's at the substation where the Nord Stream pipeline connects with the pipe that runs under the Baltic Sea," Charley said. "There will be guards on the gate. I sent another former Navy SEAL to assist you in breaching the facility. As you're in Germany and they are considered allies, we couldn't risk sending in a large team to recover Alex. I urge you not to take any more lives than are necessary. I'd prefer no lives were lost in this effort."

"Understood," Striker said as he reached the vehicle. He didn't like going into a hot situation with someone he hadn't worked with before but, since the man was a former SEAL, he could make it work. He might even know the guy. The Navy SEAL community was a small, tight-knit community of highly skilled operatives.

He opened the passenger door of the sports car and folded himself into the seat. He turned to the man behind the steering wheel and held out his hand. "Nice ride. Dane Ryan. My teammates called me Striker."

The man looked familiar in the light from the dash. He shook Striker's hand. "Adam Nichols. I think we've been on a mission together… Afghanistan, maybe?"

Striker nodded. "Been a few days, but I believe you're right." He dropped the man's hand and turned to the road ahead.

Adam handed him a tracking device.

Striker studied it eagerly, feeling just a little bit closer to rescuing Alex just by seeing on the map where she was located. The device was new and appeared expensive. "How long have you worked for Charley?"

"Not long, and I don't work for her anymore. I

only agreed to this mission to help out a fellow frogman."

"Have you actually met her?"

Adam shifted gears and hit the accelerator hard. "No. It's all smoke and mirrors. I didn't like all the secrecy. I'd refused to work with her again until she called and said a Navy SEAL was in trouble. Otherwise, I'd have told her to go fuck herself."

"Bad experience?"

"Not really. I just don't trust her. I like to look into the eyes of the person I'm working with. She doesn't give you that opportunity. And it's creepy as hell the way she knows everything about you and your movements."

Striker nodded. "I get that. But I'm glad she sent someone to assist me on this mission. What do we have to work with?"

"You're already set with comm. I've been listening in on Charley's sitrep. In the trunk, we have everything we might need, including weapons, camouflage, C4, duct tape and zip ties. Like Charley said, we can't go in shooting everything that moves. We're to get in, extract our target and get out with as little commotion as we can manage. From what we understand, the facility is rigged with an extensive video surveillance system. Charley's working to shut that down before we arrive. Apparently, their transfer system has been compromised, and the flow of natural gas has come to a complete halt."

"Then they'll be all hands on deck. That should make it more difficult to get in."

Adam nodded. "We just have to get past the gate guards. Once inside, we can use the C4 to handle any door locks." He reached behind the seat, pulled out a handgun and passed it to Striker. "In case you have no other choice."

Striker inspected the weapon in the light from the dash. The 9 mm Glock was a pistol he was familiar with. The magazine was loaded and ready to go.

"How far is this place?" Striker asked.

"About twenty minutes. It's located on the coast. We can park a mile away and go in on foot or take our chances and drive right up to the gate. The car will get their attention."

"Let's do a combination of the two alternatives. I don't want to waste time going in on foot. You can let me out a few yards ahead of the gate. While you distract the guard with the Ferrari, I'll take him out." He held up his hands. "Let me rephrase. I'll subdue him. You can be ready with the duct tape and zip ties."

Adam grinned. "Deal. It pays to demand a cool car."

Thankfully, darkness had descended on

northern Germany, giving them the concealment they'd need to infiltrate the facility.

A couple miles from their destination, Adam pulled the sports car off the road, popped the trunk and got out. They pulled on black coveralls with multiple pockets located on the sleeves and pant legs. They had a choice of camouflage sticks to blacken their faces or ski masks. Both men chose the camo sticks and quickly painted their faces and hands so that they wouldn't stand out in the darkness. They added black body armor vests and stuffed what they needed into the pockets on the vest and in the coveralls.

"How did Charley get her hands on C4 and detonators?" Striker asked.

"How does Charley do anything?" Adam responded. "Her canned response is that she has contacts. Legal or otherwise, she gets the job done."

Striker shoved a small brick of the clay-like explosives into his vest along with a detonator and trigger device. He clipped a smoke grenade to a loop and added a couple of magazines for the handgun. After staring longingly at a submachine gun and an AR 15 rifle equipped with sights, he passed over those for duct tape, zip ties and a Ka-Bar knife.

Once they were set, they climbed back into the Ferrari and drove to within a couple hundred yards of the facility.

The cellphone interface in the Ferrari rang. Adam pressed the button to receive the call. "Video surveillance system has been disengaged," Charley reported.

"Good," Adam said. "We're going in."

Adam slowed enough for Striker to jump out, and then continued to the gate, moving slowly enough Striker could catch up quickly.

Striker jogged along, checking his equipment for noise and securing anything that might alert the guard to his approach. He swung wide of the road, crossed through a field and eased up to the guard shack at the gate as Adam slowed the Ferrari to a stop.

The guard stepped out.

Adam whispered into Striker's earbud. "Only one guard."

As the guard addressed Adam, Striker eased up behind him and grabbed him in a headlock, applying enough pressure to cut off the man's air long enough for him to pass out, but not to kill the man. He checked for a pulse. The guy would live. Before the guard could fully recover, Striker secured the man's wrists and ankles with zip ties and slapped a length of duct tape over his mouth. Then he dragged him behind the guard shack and left him lying on the ground. The entire effort took less than three minutes.

While he'd secured the guard, Adam had opened the gate and driven the Ferrari through.

Striker climbed into the Ferrari, and Adam drove toward the blip on the handheld tracking device. The closer they came to the blinking dot, the faster Striker's heart beat.

No one stepped out to stop them as they neared a building at the center of the massive facility.

Adam parked the Ferrari to the side of the building, out of sight of the main entrance.

Both men climbed out and found a side door that was likely used as an emergency exit and was otherwise barred as an entry point.

It would work perfectly for their entrance into the building. Based on the tracking device, Alex was somewhere inside.

Adam pulled off a section of the C4 and weighed it in his hand. As a Navy SEAL, they'd worked with explosives enough to know how much to use to breach a lock versus how much was needed to blow the building apart. He pressed the C4 against the locking mechanism on the door.

Striker mashed the detonator into the clay-like explosives and nodded. "Ready?"

Adam nodded, and the men stepped around the corner.

Striker rested his finger on the button, ready to set the plan in motion. Depending on where the majority of people were congregating, a small explosion might not alert all inside to an attack. That's what he hoped for. If every damned person inside decided to take up arms and fight, so be it. Striker wouldn't leave without Alex.

ALEX LIFTED her chin and turned to Baranovsky. "If she shoots me in the face, you won't have access to the software on that flash drive. It's encrypted with biometric software. I'm the only one who has access."

Baranovsky lunged for Natalya's arm, knocking the barrel to the side just as Natalya pulled the trigger.

The bullet hit the man on Alex's left. He jerked backward, releasing his hold on her arm.

Apparently shocked by the fact Natalya had fired the weapon inside the control room, the other man holding her arm also loosened his grip.

Alex jerked free and ran for the nearest door. As she reached it, she looked back to find Baranovsky struggling to free the gun from Natalya's hands.

The weapon went off. Baranovsky fell to his knees and toppled forward, the flash drive flying from his hand.

Natalya crossed to where it landed and stepped on it with her high-heeled shoe, crushing it beneath her.

Alex's chest tightened. Her parents had given

their lives for what was contained on that flash drive.

Natalya turned toward Alex and aimed the gun.

A muffled boom sounded somewhere above. At first, Alex thought it was Natalya firing at her. A loud bang behind her sent her diving through the door as pieces of the wall above her fell into her hair. She passed the elevator, knowing it would take too long for that door to open and close again. Natalya would be within firing range too soon.

Alex ran toward a sign that indicated stairs. She heard footsteps behind her. As she pushed through the door to a stairwell, she shot a glance over her shoulder. The man who hadn't been shot was running toward her. Natalya emerged into the hallway behind him, aimed her weapon and fired over the man's shoulder at Alex.

The bullet hit the wall above her head. Alex let the door swing closed behind her as she raced up the stairs. Since she'd been brought in with a bag over her head, she had no idea how to get out of the building or where exactly she was. Her primary focus was to get away from Natalya and the men working for her. She couldn't avenge her parents if the other woman put a bullet through her first.

The stairs led to another level of the facility, opening up into an area with a metal catwalk that crossed over huge pipes and machines below. Across the maze of catwalks, Alex spotted the elevator shaft and the car rising up from the floor below. Footsteps pounded on the wire mesh of the catwalk behind her.

Alex ran to a set of stairs and climbed up to another level of metal steps. The man behind her followed. Natalya exited the elevator on the level below and stood waiting for a clear shot.

Alex refused to give it to her. She hid behind a massive column that stretched from the bottom of the facility through the roof. She couldn't keep running or Natalya would eventually get the drop on her. Alex waited on the other side of the column. She had to deal with the man following her before she could find her way out of the building. If it meant going through Natalya, so be it. After all, the woman was the one she'd been searching for. She'd freely admitted she'd had Alex's parents killed.

Anger burned deep in Alex's chest, but she wouldn't let it control her. She channeled the adrenaline into action.

When the man following her ran around the column, Alex was ready. She bent low and rammed into him, driving him backward. He slammed into the catwalk railing and tipped backward.

Alex gave him the extra push needed to send him flying over the rail. He crashed to the concrete floor below and lay still.

Which left her with one woman carrying a gun

between her and getting the hell out of whatever building they'd brought her to.

At least, she thought that was all there was between her and the exit. She didn't know what other security was in place.

"You might as well come out," Natalya called, her voice echoing against the pipes and walls. "There is only one way out of this building, and my people are waiting outside.

Alex didn't respond. Her best bet was to move quietly and sneak up behind the woman. It was hard to do on the metal mesh of the catwalk, but she couldn't remain hidden behind the column indefinitely. Looking around, she found a metal ladder that led to the level below, and it was behind the column which would provide the concealment she'd need to make the descent without Natalya shooting her before she reached the bottom. Alex swung her leg over the rail, held onto the sides of the ladder and eased her way down as quietly as she could.

When she reached the bottom, she stepped off onto a solid floor. Before she could turn, the barrel of a gun pressed against her throat. The scent of perfume wafted around her.

Natalya.

"You can't be allowed to leave this facility alive," she said. "You were supposed to die two years ago."

Alex cursed beneath her breath. If she so much

as flinched, the woman would pull the trigger and that would be the end of her search for vengeance.

"You have been the one loose thread that needed to be tied. I wasn't sure you were a threat until Baranovsky stole you away from the conference. I figured he knew you had what your parents stole from me, and he was going to use it to cheat me out of what he owes me."

Alex wanted to take this woman out, but Natalya had the upper hand with a gun pointed at her and her finger on the trigger. "You're both thieves and deserve each other," Alex said through gritted teeth.

Natalya snorted. "Your parents were no better. They stole from me. For that, they had to die."

"You destroyed the flash drive. I have nothing to hold against you."

"Maybe so, but now you know who I am."

"And who is that?" Alex said. "The person holding companies and nations hostage with ransomware? You prey on others."

"I prey on stupid people."

"You put people at risk of dying. Without natural gas, many will freeze to death."

"All they have to do is pay, and it's theirs," she said.

Alex glared at her. "It's blackmail, extortion."

"It's business," she said. "My business."

"And illegal."

"You do what you have to do to make a living," Natalya said. "Now that the pirated copy is destroyed I have no use for you."

"Then let me go," Alex said.

Natalya shook her head. "Can't. You know too much."

"And so do we," said a deep, familiar voice said from behind Natalya. "Put down the gun."

Natalya grabbed a handful of Alex's hair and yanked her around, using her as a shield.

Alex's heart leaped when she looked past Natalya to see Striker with a gun in his hand.

Natalya laughed. "You have to go through her to get to me. And I'll put a bullet in her before you can pull the trigger."

Alex had more than she could stand of the Russian mafia interpreter bitch. She reached up, grabbed the woman's hand with the gun and yanked it down.

Natalya pulled the trigger. The bullet went wide.

Alex turned and wrestled the woman for the gun. She'd be damned if she let Natalya get away with anything else. She was going down. Now. Today.

But damn, the woman had a strong grip on the gun.

CHAPTER 12

STRIKER RUSHED toward the two women struggling for domination over the gun.

Alex and Natalya spun, the gun pointing outward toward Striker and Adam, and fired another round.

They dropped to the ground.

"I'm. So. Over. This," Alex said between clenched teeth. She grabbed Natalya's arms and rolled backward, planted her feet in Natalya's gut and flipped her into the air.

The other woman landed hard on her back, the gun dropping from her hand.

Alex leaped to her feet and rushed toward Natalya.

Before Alex reached her, Natalya grasped the gun and pointed it at Alex.

Striker dove for Alex, knocking her out of range

of Natalya's aim, and in the process, took the bullet meant for Alex.

Another shot rang out. Natalya's eyes rounded, and her mouth formed an O. The gun fell from her fingers, and she looked down at her chest where blood spread across her royal purple dress. She looked across at Alex and Striker and cried, "Noooo."

Natalya fell backward and lay still.

Adam crossed to the woman, holstering his weapon. He bent and felt the base of her throat. After a moment, he looked up. "She's dead. Time to leave."

Striker clutched a hand to his side as he pushed to his feet. He held out his other hand to help Alex to her feet.

She came up frowning. "You're bleeding."

He took her hand. "I'll survive," he said. "The main thing is to get the hell out of here before the entire German police force and army come down on us."

"We're in Germany?" Alex laughed. "I knew we were in a gas facility, but I wasn't sure what country. They knocked me out. I don't know for how long."

"Bastards," Striker swore. "Come on. There's plane waiting for us. But you'll have to share a seat with me in the getaway car."

"I guess I didn't think that detail through,"

Adam said. "Doesn't matter as long as we can get to the airport fast."

Striker laughed. "I think you can handle that." He took Alex's hand and led her through the maze of corridors.

An alarm went off, and security personnel rushed through the building, heading for the control room. Several times Alex, Striker and Adam had to duck into a dark corner to avoid being seen. Soon, they arrived at the door Adam and Striker had destroyed the lock on.

Once outside, they ran for the Ferrari. Striker got into the passenger seat and pulled Alex onto his lap.

Adam slid behind the wheel, revved the engine and shot through the compound to the gate they'd left open. A security guard was just pulling the gate shut and was halfway there when the Ferrari flew through the narrow gap and out onto the street.

Adam touched a button on the steering wheel.

"Did you get her?" Charley's voice sounded on the car's speaker.

"We did," Adam responded.

"Alex, the voice you hear is Charley, my boss," Striker said. "Charley brought us here to get you back."

"Thank you, Charley," Alex said.

"What about the flash drive?" Charley asked.

Alex answered. "Natalya destroyed it. She said it

was a pirated copy of the ransomware software she used to shut down the Nord Stream pipeline."

"The European Union is in an uproar over the cessation of the flow of natural gas into Europe," Charley said. "Fortunately, when you had the flash drive connected to Striker's computer, we downloaded a copy. All we need is Ms. Sokolov present to decrypt it with biometrics.

"I have a pilot on standby to fly you all back to the States. A representative of the CIA cyber security unit will meet you at Dulles International Airport."

They made the twenty-minute drive back to the airport in twelve, racing past the German Polizei.

As Charley had indicated, a plane sat waiting for them on the tarmac.

Adam left the Ferrari beside it. "I love this car," he said as he leaped out of it and shut the door.

"Maybe if you come back to work for Charley, she'll give you one of your own," Striker said.

"Not a chance. Not until she reveals who she is," Adam said. "Even then, I'm not convinced."

Striker led Alex up into the plane and settled in the seat beside her. "You might as well get comfortable; it's a long flight back to DC."

She nodded and reached for his hand. "Thanks for coming to my rescue. How did you find me?"

He squeezed her fingers gently. "Charley. She

had the foresight to plant a tracker on you. Adam's not a fan, but I'm warming up to her."

"Will you get to meet her in person in DC?" Alex asked.

Adam snorted in the seat in front of them. "Doubt it. She likes her anonymity."

Alex frowned. "Do they have a first aid kit on board?"

A man dressed in a business suit climbed into the plane and closed the hatch. He brought with him a box with a red cross on it. "I believe you might need this. Do you require assistance with it?"

"I'll assist him." Alex took the box from the attendant.

Striker removed his shirt, wincing as he did.

Alex opened the first aid kit and pulled out gauze and alcohol.

"It's just a flesh wound," Striker said.

"He's a SEAL. That's what they all say," Adam said. "He's probably mortally wounded, but he won't admit it."

"Seriously," Striker said. "It barely nicked me."

"Hush and let me clean the wound," Alex said. "Then I'll be the judge of it."

"I like a woman who takes charge," Striker said with a grin.

"Must be why you like Charley," Adam grumbled.

"And I like a woman who fights for what she

believes in and for the people she cares about," Striker tipped up Alex's chin. "What are you going to do now that your quest is over?"

She shrugged. "I don't know. My parents worked for the CIA. At one time, I thought about applying there. But now, I'm not certain they'd have me."

"What about the interpreting gig?" Striker asked. "There's a demand for interpreters who speak Russian and German."

"Good thing to know I have options." She sighed. "I feel a little lost, like a woman without a country. I don't even have my backpack that carries everything I own. It was my world. I could go anywhere with it."

"We can contact the Hotel Le Negresco and have them send it to you," Striker suggested.

"That would be nice." Alex finished cleaning his injury. "You're right. It's just a flesh wound. You'll be healed in no time." She applied a bandage and smiled. "Better?"

"Much." Striker pulled his damaged shirt back over his head and settled into his seat. "Looks like we'll have decisions to make when this is all over."

Alex leaned back, nodded and closed her eyes. "Tomorrow will come soon enough for decisions."

"Sleep," Striker said.

She leaned her head onto his shoulder.

He pressed his lips to her forehead. "I hope one

of your decisions is to spend some time with me," he whispered.

"I'd like that very much. Are you sure you want to be with me?"

"More than anything," he said.

"Could you two shut up?" Adam grumbled. "Trying to sleep here."

Striker cupped her cheek and then pressed his lips to hers in a brief kiss. "See you when we wake up on the other side of the pond."

ONE MONTH *later*

Alex smiled as she sat beside the pool in her own backyard in San Diego, California. She'd always wanted to visit the city and never thought she would actually get to live there. But here she was, in her own home, with a view of the bay in front of her.

After she'd met with the CIA and helped them get into the software her parents had stolen from Natalya, the cyber security unit was able to reverse the damage the ransomware had created for Nord Stream.

The cyber security team worked day and night to make it happen and had the natural gas flowing again within forty-eight hours of it being shut down. They'd also learned from the software how to safeguard computer systems against future attacks. All because Alex's parents had sacrificed their lives to help others.

After Baranovsky's and Natalya's deaths, Anatoly Petrov was able to convince the other members of the Energy Summit that no more siphoning would occur. He would put security measures in place to keep it from happening again. With that promise, he got the members to sign off on the construction of the pipeline.

"Can I get you another glass of wine?" Striker asked as he set his beer on the table between their two lounge chairs.

"No, thank you," she said. "I'm still sipping this one. What time did Adam and Angela say they were getting here?"

"In about an hour." Striker settled in the chair beside her and reached for her hand. "Why?"

She smiled. "I was just thinking…"

"About?"

"About how good it would feel to make love in the water." She hadn't been thinking that, but now that she had, heat coiled low in her belly. "Know anyone who would care to join me?" she asked as she rose from her lounge chair and unhooked the back of her bikini top, letting the straps slide down her arms.

"I could think of a few." Striker was off his chair in a second, pulling his shirt up over his head and tossing it onto his chair.

Alex shimmied out of her bikini bottoms and stepped to the edge of the pool. Her backyard had a tall privacy fence on both sides and was perched on the side of a hill overlooking the bay in the distance.

Ever since Charley and the CIA had set her up with a new identity, passport and social security number, she'd finally started living her life. The best part of it was the time she spent with Striker, getting to know him better and making love with him every chance she could.

He had performed other shorter jobs for Charley and was happy to be employed, even if he wasn't thrilled about his boss being more or less a ghost. The work was rewarding and for the greater good.

They'd seen each other throughout the month, getting to know each other better. Alex wasn't sure they were ready to commit to marriage, but she would consider it if Striker asked. She knew in her heart they would have the kind of love her mother and father had enjoyed. And that made her happier than she'd been in a long time.

She was even happier when they made love.

Striker shucked his shorts and joined her at the edge of the pool.

"I like that you're adventurous," he said, taking her into his arms.

"I like that you like when I am." She leaned up on her toes and brushed her lips against his.

"We have fifty-nine minutes until our guests arrive," Striker reminded her.

She grinned. "Then we'd better get going."

Striker bent and scooped her up into his arms and walked into the water that had been warmed by the sun. Once there, they made love in the near weightlessness, laughing at how they had to cling to each other throughout to keep from floating away.

When they had each had their fill, they surfaced and lay in the sun on the same lounge chair to dry, holding hands and touching each other until they made love again.

Yeah, Alex was well on her way to trusting this man with her heart. And she was already there in love with him.

"Hey," he leaned up on one elbow and pressed a kiss to the tip of her nose, "what are you thinking about?"

She wrapped her arms around his neck and pulled his head down so that she could kiss him. "I'm thinking that I love you."

His eyes widened. "Love? As in the big L word?"

She nodded. "The big L."

He gazed into her eyes. "Does that mean you trust me now?"

Her eyes narrowed playfully. "I don't know about that, but you're definitely growing on me."

"Good, because that makes it easier," he said.

Her brow wrinkled. "Easier?"

He nodded. "Easier for me to do this." He rolled off the lounge chair, reached for his shorts and removed a box from inside. "Alex, I'm pretty sure I first fell in love with you when you flipped Anatoly Petrov over your head at the Energy Summit in Nice. I'd never met a woman who could so effectively put a man in his place."

Her heart filled to overflowing. "You love me?"

He nodded and opened the box to display a diamond ring. "I love you enough to risk my heart and bare my soul to ask you to do me the honor of becoming my wife. I promise to love you and cherish you for the rest of my life. Please, say yes."

She laughed, flung her arms around his neck and answered, "Yes!"

He gathered her naked body in his arms and sealed their promise to each other with a kiss.

When they finally came up for air, he whispered into her ear. "There's only one more thing we need to do."

"And what's that?" she asked, so happy she thought her heart might burst.

Striker winked. "We need to get dressed. I think I heard a car pull up in the driveway. I can't wait to tell Adam and Angela that you and I are getting married."

"I can't wait to get married," Alex said. "I'm ready to spend the rest of my life loving you."

"And I'm ready to love you for the rest of my life."

She smiled. "We just had to go halfway around the world to find each other."

Striker held her close. "I'd do it all again."

SHADOW IN THE DESERT

BECCA JAMESON

Shadow in the Desert
By Becca Jameson

CHAPTER 1

AJAX WAS RUNNING a few minutes late, so he took the stairs two at a time instead of the elevator. He was only going to the second floor of this D.C. office building, and he wasn't at all sure why he even gave a fuck if he was late.

He had no idea who he was meeting with or why. In fact, he wasn't sure what compelled him to bother showing up today, except that he had nothing else to do, so why not?

As he pushed through the door that led from the stairwell into the hallway, he paused to catch his breath and straighten his shirt. He hated that he was slightly out of breath because he'd let himself lounge a bit too much for the past few months. He was uncomfortable in his clothes for the same reason. His khaki pants were a bit tight and his blue button-down shirt was annoying his neck. He wore it untucked because…well, mostly because again, he didn't give a fuck.

He'd put a half-assed effort into looking presentable, but that had not included a shave or a haircut, nor had it included a tie.

He shouldn't have felt uncomfortable dressed like this. He'd spent seventeen years in the Navy for heaven's sake. He was used to being starched and straight. But it had been three months since he'd last donned his uniform, so he was out of practice.

Who was he kidding? For most of those three months, he'd lounged around in his sister's den wearing sweatpants and T-shirts. He'd drank far more than his share of beer, and he shuddered to think how many bottles of Jack.

"What the fuck am I even doing here?" he muttered to himself as he drew in a breath and headed for office number 212.

It didn't take long to find. It was three doors down on the right. He narrowed his gaze as he found the number on the door. Nothing else. No business name, nothing. The other offices in the hallway had placards on the door indicating what company they were.

For a moment, he stood rooted to his spot, hands on his hips, staring at the door and then glancing around. If there had been another human in the hallway, he would have asked them if they knew anything about this office. There was no window, so he couldn't even peer inside.

Unease crept up his spine, causing him to lift an arm and rub the back of his neck. "Shit," he muttered. "This is by far the stupidest thing I have ever done." He didn't have nearly enough details about why he was here to have believed it was legit. Hell, he'd been hungover when he answered the phone. The only reason why he doubted it was a trap was that it was the middle of D.C. This was a busy office building. What could possibly go wrong?

He chuckled as he thought of the possibilities. Considering how fucked-up his life currently was, anything could go wrong.

You're here, dumb as the decision might have been. Just open the damn door.

He patted his right hip where he'd worn a weapon nearly every second of every day for many years until recently. It wasn't there now. He didn't have a weapon on him this morning at all.

With a deep breath, he pulled the door open, holding on to it as he stepped halfway into the room. In his mind, he figured if he didn't like what he saw on the other side, he could step back out, let the door close, and walk away.

If whatever was behind the door was nefarious, on the other hand, he would probably be dead before he had a chance to retreat.

The room was small. Nothing more than a conference table with six chairs and a phone in the middle, but that's not what mattered. That wasn't what stopped Ajax in his tracks and took his breath away. "Holy mother of God," he stated as he released the door, no longer caring if it shut at his back.

The man standing on the other side of the room lifted his gaze and gasped.

For a moment, they simply stared at each other. Not a single sound could be heard except the beating of Ajax's heart in his ears. "Fuck me. Ryker?" He would know his foster brother anywhere. He didn't need verification. Except since he knew Ryker was dead, it was a bit difficult to believe his eyes.

"Ajax?" Ryker took a hesitant step forward. "Is that really you?" It occurred to Ajax that Ryker thought he was dead also.

Ajax took two huge steps forward at the same time as Ryker, and they collided in what could be described as a manly hug, if it weren't for the fact that Ajax's throat was clogged with emotion.

"I thought..." Ryker's voice was tight, and Ajax understood.

"They said you were dead," the men choked out in unison.

When they leaned back, they held each other by

the shoulders and stared into each other's eyes. "What the fuck?" Ryker said.

"I was going to say the same thing."

"Where the fuck have you been?" Ryker asked.

"My sister's. In Tennessee. You?"

"Mom and Dad's place in Indiana." Ryker released Ajax to rub his forehead. "What the fuck is going on?"

"Not a damn clue. Do you suppose the entire team is coming here?"

The door opened behind Ajax and he spun around, half expecting to see Keebler or Pitbull or any of the other members of their SEAL squad.

That is most definitely not what happened. The newest addition was a woman. Prim. Perfectly put together. Ajax scanned her from the feet up. Four-inch heels. Gray pencil skirt that reached her knees. White blouse. Flawless pale skin. Sleek black hair in a tidy bun. Green eyes. She had two manila folders tucked under one elbow.

She wasted no time, immediately holding a hand out to Ajax. "Mr. Cassman." He shook her hand, uncertain what to say. Her voice didn't match the sultry voice he'd heard on the phone. When he released her grip, she reached for Ryker. "Mr. Tufano."

"How do you know who we are? And who the fuck are you?" Ryker asked.

"My name is Serena."

"I was told to meet with a man named Charlie," Ajax stated, glancing at Ryker who nodded agreement. He'd been told the same thing.

Serena smiled politely. "She couldn't make it." She reached toward the center of the table and dragged the phone toward the edge. "She'll be joining us by speakerphone."

"Charley is a woman?" Ajax asked for clarification. He wasn't usually such a sexist ass, but he'd wrongly assumed... *Charley, not Charlie.*

Serena lifted a brow. "Yes. You have a problem with women?"

Ajax lifted both brows and then stroked his beard. He felt defensive. "Not at all." *Especially not you.* This entire situation was ten ways of fucked-up, but Serena wasn't one of them. She was cool, confident, and feisty. It was absurd that his cock took notice because he had about a thousand questions to ask her. Now was not the time to flirt.

"You didn't answer my question," Ryker stated, his voice firm, no-nonsense. That hadn't changed. "Who are you?"

"I told you."

"Gonna need more than a name, sweetheart," Ryker stated.

Serena flinched, narrowing her gaze at him. "I'm not your sweetheart, and that's all you need to know." She picked up the phone, dialed a number so fast that Ajax couldn't see the digits, and then pressed a button to put it on speaker.

As the phone rang, Serena pointed toward the chairs. "Have a seat, gentlemen."

Ajax shot Ryker a narrow look before responding. The two of them had known each other since Ajax moved into the foster home where Ryker had already been living at age twelve. They'd been separated only once since then, and that had been for the last three months. They didn't need words to convey what they were thinking. "We'll stand," Ajax stated, planting his feet wider and crossing his arms defiantly. He wanted some fucking answers and fast.

Serena shrugged. "Suit yourselves." She made no move to sit either. Nor did she seem remotely bothered by the high heels she stood in. It looked like she wore them often. Every movement she made indicated she was more comfortable in heels than any other footwear.

"Hello?" came an unknown female voice.

"Charley, this is Serena. You are on speakerphone. I have Mr. Cassman and Mr. Tufano here with me."

"Good." The silky, smooth pitch of her voice confirmed she was female.

Ajax narrowed his gaze, glaring at the phone.

"Mind telling us what this is all about and do you know why on earth we were both told the other was dead? And while you're at it, where is the rest of our team?" Ryker demanded.

"I'm going to answer all of your questions, gentlemen," Charley responded. "Has my assistant offered you a beverage? This is going to take a few minutes. You might want to get comfortable."

Ajax scowled. "We don't need anything to drink. We need answers."

"Look. I'm not the bad guy here. My goal is to help you. You were wronged. My intention is to right that wrong."

"Who do you work for?" Ryker asked.

"Can't tell you that. What you need to know is that I'm on your side. I know everything that happened to the two of you and the rest of your team. I'd like to hire you to do a covert job."

Ajax dropped his arms and leaned forward, setting his palms on the table so he could lean in closer to the phone. "Hire us? Why would we want to work for you? We know nothing about you, and frankly, right now I'm two seconds from pulling the phone cord out of the wall and leaving this room. So, you better give us some answers fast before I lose my cool."

The woman sighed. "The reason you're going to take me up on my offer is because I'm going to make you a deal you can't refuse, and the job I need you to do is to go back into Ethiopia and rescue the rest of your team."

Ajax gasped as he glanced at Ryker. "You're telling me the rest of our guys are still in fucking Ethiopia?"

"Yes. My intel suggests they're alive. I'm still gathering data about their specific location, but I'm expecting to make contact with my source so we can get this ball rolling in two weeks."

Ajax stared at the phone. This was insane. How could he possibly trust this woman? "Who are you?"

"You can call me Charley. Beyond that, I can't tell you."

Ajax jerked his gaze toward Serena. "My partner and I could easily overtake this woman you've sent and force her to talk."

Serena gasped and took a step back, the first evidence that she was flappable.

Charley sighed again. "She knows nothing. It won't do you any good."

Ajax gritted his teeth and closed his eyes, his face dipping toward the floor.

"Listen to me," Charley demanded. "I know everything that happened to you. More than either of you know. You were on a mission, you had the green light, you surrounded the target, and then you closed in. There was an explosion. The building blew to rubble. The two of you were knocked off your feet and thrown backward, landing hard in the street several yards from where you'd been standing. You were both knocked unconscious in the blast."

"Why on earth was I told the entire team was dead and I was the lone survivor?" Ajax asked.

"Because someone higher up needed to cover their own ass."

Ajax shoved away from the table and took a few steps back, leaning against the wall for support. He ran a hand through his hair, hair that was in desperate need of a cut. "How do you know all of this?"

"I have my ways."

Ajax groaned.

"What happened to the rest of the team if they didn't die in the explosion?" Ryker asked.

"No one was in that rubble. None of you had breached the building yet. You two were the only ones knocked unconscious. Everyone else was taken hostage in the ambush. Your backup team was moving in fast, so the rebels had no choice but to evacuate and leave your bodies behind. They probably weren't certain if you were alive or dead, but in any case, they didn't have the time to take two unconscious bodies."

"Unbelievable," Ajax murmured.

"I agree. Whoever fucked up this mission went to a lot of trouble to clean up after themselves."

"If the backup team rescued us, why haven't we heard from any of them?"

"They are still active in the mission, and they've been told neither of you survived. After loading you two into the helicopter, they never saw you again."

Ryker cleared his throat. "This is insane. Both of us were told the rest of the team was dead. Who could be that cruel?"

Ajax agreed. It had been the most hellacious three months of his life. He'd spent it believing not only his entire team was dead, but that it included Ryker. A man he'd considered a brother since they met when Ajax was twelve.

Ajax had yet to go home to Indiana to face the foster parents who brought him into manhood because he couldn't stand the idea of confronting the heaviness in his soul. On top of that, he was too embarrassed. He'd been told the reason that mission failed—the reason Ryker had died—was because he hadn't followed protocol. He'd been fucking led to believe that he had disgraced his team and the SEALs. He had been discharged "other than honorably." Returning to face his foster parents was the last thing he'd wanted to do.

"I don't know the answer to that yet, but believe me, I'm working on it. In the meantime, I'm hiring you two to go back and get your team."

Ajax flinched. "Hiring? What if we decline."

"You won't."

Serena set the two folders she was carrying on

the table, separated them, and eased them across
the surface, one toward each man. A phoenix stared
back at him as though the ancient Egyptian bird
could see all the way to his damaged soul...daring
him to look inside.

Ryker opened his first and after a moment, he
whistled between his teeth. "That's a lot of money."

"Yes. You have a unique set of skills, not to
mention motivation."

Ajax opened his folder and lifted both brows.
Ryker wasn't kidding. He could do a lot with that
kind of money. "You realize I've been discharged. I
no longer work for the US Navy. Who the heck are
we working for?"

"Me."

"And you aren't going to tell us who the hell you
are?"

"No. It's safer this way."

"For us or for you?"

"Yes."

Great.

Ryker groaned.

Ajax turned to look at him, lifting a brow. They
were either in this together or not at all.

"Fuck," Ryker muttered.

Ajax agreed. It wasn't as though they could tell
this woman they would not be willing to go in and
rescue their own men. He turned back to face the
phone. "What's the plan?"

"Pull your shit together, lay off the cookies, and be prepared to travel in two weeks."

"Who's paying for all this?" Ajax asked.

"I am."

"How will we know where to go or what to do?"

"Serena will be traveling with you. She'll be told when and where to meet up with my contact when you arrive."

"What?" all three yelled at once.

For Ajax, the thought of this soft woman in the pencil skirt traveling to fucking Ethiopia with him was preposterous. She obviously worked hard to be taken seriously. Standing tall. Keeping her expression tight and serious. All business. But his instinct told him she was more like a dandelion underneath the fake exterior.

That wasn't the most shocking part of Charley's announcement, however. The part that made Ajax lift both brows and glance at Serena was that she too was obviously blindsided by this news.

"Charley," Serena began, "at no time did you mention me traveling with these gentlemen." She was clearly just as uninterested as Ajax was. Traveling to Ethiopia was dangerous under normal circumstances. He would have his guard up the entire time. And that would be when he was in populated areas surrounded by civilians.

As soon as he left civilization to hunt down his squad, the last thing he'd need was to worry about this feather of a woman. No way. Not a chance. "That's a dealbreaker," he told Charley.

Serena flinched and shot him a narrowed look that could have melted a cast-iron pan. She may not have had any intentions of going either, but she sure didn't like the decision coming from him.

"Nonnegotiable. Serena goes with you. I'll overnight you the details in a few days. Plane tickets and all the information you'll need to get started. When you arrive, you'll stay in a hotel in Addis Ababa the first night. After that, you'll meet up with my contact and be given further instructions."

Ryker slapped his hands onto the table again, fingers wide, fingertips white from gripping the surface. "How do we know this isn't a trap intended to get both of us killed so that whoever fucked up this mission can wipe their hands clean of possible loose ends?"

Serena leaned forward and pushed the top piece of paper in the open manila folder to one side, her fingers moving slowly to reveal the second page.

Ajax's breath hitched and caught. "Motherfucker," he breathed out. He yanked the entire stack of pages off the table and started flipping through them while Ryker did the same with his set of documents.

"Fuck," Ryker muttered.

The first several pages were pictures of the rest

of their squad. They were grainy and black and white, but there was no mistaking the images of their comrades. Recent images. Their brothers looked like shit. Three months of neglect.

Fuck.

Whoever this Charley woman was, she had them both by the balls. There wasn't a chance in hell either of them would leave men behind for any reason. Even if Charley was fucking with them and intended to have the two of them killed the moment they stepped off the plane, it was a risk Ajax would have to take. And he knew Ryker would too.

Plus, why send Serena with them if Charley intended to have them both killed? That part made no sense.

Apparently, Ajax was headed back to Ethiopia.

MORE SHADOW SEALS

Cat Johnson *Shadow Pawn*
Elle James *Shadow Assassin*
Becca Jameson *Shadow in the Desert*
KaLyn Cooper *Shadow in the Mountain (08/10/21)*
Donna Michaels *Shadow of a Chance (08/31/21)*
J.M. Madden *Shadow of the Moon (09/21/21)*
Sharon Hamilton *Shadow of the Heart (10/12/21)*
Desiree Holt *Shadow Defender (01/04/22)*
Elaine Levine *Not My Shadow (01/25/22)*
Abbie Zanders *Cast in Shadow (02/15/22)*

Shadow SEALs on Amazon

Shadow SEALs Facebook Reader Group

Interested in more military romance stories?
Subscribe to my newsletter and receive the
Military Heroes Box Set
Subscribe Here

ABOUT THE AUTHOR

ELLE JAMES also writing as MYLA JACKSON is a *New York Times* and *USA Today* Bestselling author of books including cowboys, intrigues and paranormal adventures that keep her readers on the edges of their seats. When she's not at her computer, she's traveling, snow skiing, boating, or riding her ATV, dreaming up new stories. Learn more about Elle James at www.ellejames.com

Website | Facebook | Twitter | GoodReads | Newsletter | BookBub | Amazon

Or visit her alter ego Myla Jackson at mylajackson.com
Website | Facebook | Twitter | Newsletter

Follow Me!
www.ellejames.com
ellejames@ellejames.com

Warrior's Resolve (#5)

The Billionaire Husband Test (#1)

The Billionaire Cinderella Test (#2)

The Billionaire Bride Test (#3)

The Billionaire Daddy Test (#4)

The Billionaire Matchmaker Test (#5)

The Billionaire Glitch Date (#6)

The Billionaire Perfect Date (#7) coming soon

The Billionaire Replacement Date (#8) coming soon

The Billionaire Wedding Date (#9) coming soon

Ballistic Cowboy

Hot Combat (#1)

Hot Target (#2)

Hot Zone (#3)

Hot Velocity (#4)

Cajun Magic Mystery Series

Voodoo on the Bayou (#1)

Voodoo for Two (#2)

Deja Voodoo (#3)

Cajun Magic Mysteries Books 1-3

SEAL Of My Own

Navy SEAL Survival

Navy SEAL Captive

Navy SEAL To Die For

Navy SEAL Six Pack

Devil's Shroud Series

Deadly Reckoning (#1)

Deadly Engagement (#2)

Deadly Liaisons (#3)

Deadly Allure (#4)

Deadly Obsession (#5)

Deadly Fall (#6)

Covert Cowboys Inc Series

Triggered (#1)

Taking Aim (#2)

Bodyguard Under Fire (#3)

Cowboy Resurrected (#4)

Navy SEAL Justice (#5)

Navy SEAL Newlywed (#6)

High Country Hideout (#7)

Clandestine Christmas (#8)

Thunder Horse Series

Hostage to Thunder Horse (#1)

Thunder Horse Heritage (#2)

Thunder Horse Redemption (#3)

Christmas at Thunder Horse Ranch (#4)

Demon Series

Hot Demon Nights (#1)

Demon's Embrace (#2)

Tempting the Demon (#3)

Lords of the Underworld

Witch's Initiation (#1)

Witch's Seduction (#2)

The Witch's Desire (#3)

Possessing the Witch (#4)

Stealth Operations Specialists (SOS)

Nick of Time

Alaskan Fantasy

Boys Behaving Badly Anthology

Rogues (#1)

Blue Collar (#2)

Pirates (#3)

Stranded (#4)

First Responder (#5)

Blown Away

Warrior's Conquest

Enslaved by the Viking Short Story

Conquests

Smokin' Hot Firemen

Protecting the Colton Bride

Protecting the Colton Bride & Colton's Cowboy Code

Heir to Murder

Secret Service Rescue

High Octane Heroes

Haunted

Engaged with the Boss

Cowboy Brigade

Time Raiders: The Whisper

Bundle of Trouble

Killer Body

Operation XOXO

An Unexpected Clue

Baby Bling

Under Suspicion, With Child

Texas-Size Secrets

Cowboy Sanctuary

Lakota Baby

Dakota Meltdown

Beneath the Texas Moon

Made in the USA
Coppell, TX
01 July 2021

58417649R00128